"I'm not interested in getting involved with you, Drew."

"I think you are."

"Then think again," Eve advised grimly. "You really expect me to amuse you until you do decide to go back to Lottie? It's *obvious* that's what you're going to do!"

"Is that a fact?" he asked with interest.

Even he hadn't the gall to deny it, she noticed. "Of course, it'll have to be when *you* decide. I expect a man has to salvage a bit of pride in a situation like this."

"You seem to have thought this through very thoroughly."

She turned her head sharply to shut out the amused glow in his eyes. "Let me out, Drew."

"Only out of the room, sweetheart, not my life!"

KIM LAWRENCE lives on a farm in rural Wales. She runs two miles daily and finds this an excellent opportunity to unwind and seek inspiration for her writing. It also helps her keep up with her husband, two active sons and the various stray animals that have adopted them. Always a fanatical consumer of fiction, Kim is now equally enthusiastic about writing. She loves a happy ending!

MISTRESS BY MISTAKE

KIM LAWRENCE

MISTRESS MATERIAL

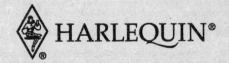

HARLEQUIN®

TORONTO • NEW YORK • LONDON
AMSTERDAM • PARIS • SYDNEY • HAMBURG
STOCKHOLM • ATHENS • TOKYO • MILAN • MADRID
PRAGUE • WARSAW • BUDAPEST • AUCKLAND

ISBN 0-373-80619-1

MISTRESS BY MISTAKE

First North American Publication 2003.

Copyright © 2002 by Kim Lawrence.

www.eHarlequin.com

Printed in U.S.A.

CHAPTER ONE

'WE DON'T have to…you know…?'

Eve took pity on the teenage youth, who was looking more like the traditional sacrificial victim by the second. 'Kiss? Definitely not,' she said firmly. A ghost of a smile touched her lips as, with an unflattering sigh of relief, he slumped farther back onto the leather Chesterfield, his thin shoulders hunched.

'Nothing personal,' he added gruffly, casting a quick glance in her direction, just to see if she was holding up to the weight of his rejection.

'Don't fret. I'll live,' she promised with a gravity that was belied by the humorous light in her wide-spaced dark brown eyes.

It said a lot about her brother's powers of persuasion, she thought, experiencing a tweak of resentful admiration for her manipulative sibling, that they were both sitting there like a pair of ill-matched bookends on Daniel Beck's parents' sofa, in Daniel Beck's parents' rather awesomely magnificent house. Eve was trying hard not to be over-awed by her surroundings. She hadn't realised until today what sort of background her brother's quiet, earnest friend came from. Everything in this magnificent house spoke of taste and money—serious money.

She doubted the black silky bias-cut creation that clung to her slim hips and thighs was the only designer label this particular sofa had seen. It was certainly the only designer label her body had ever worn—or was ever likely to for that matter!

That wasn't just because her income didn't run to such

luxuries; Eve chose her clothes for comfort rather than impact. Her wardrobe boasted one skirt, which she wheeled out for weddings, funerals and interviews with her bank manager. She probably looked just as uncomfortable as poor Daniel, who was looking—well, frankly he looked ready to bolt!

'Not long now,' she said, glancing at the chunky, utilitarian watch on her wrist—a watch that definitely didn't match her slinky outfit. Nick hadn't *exactly* said synchronise watches, but he'd still managed to instil a strong sense of edge-of-the-seat tension when he'd given his detailed instructions.

'Oh, God!'

My thought exactly! She summoned a smile that was meant to be maternal and comforting. The maternal part wasn't that difficult, chronologically a mere five years might separate her from this boy, but in every other way she felt centuries older!

'How long are your parents away for, Daniel?' I'll kill Nick for talking me into this, she decided as her high, curving cheekbones began to ache from the effort of smiling. What'll I do if he faints before they all get here? Or, worse still, throws up over the carpet—a carpet that incidentally looks far too rich and sumptuous to actually walk on. The voice of impending doom in her head was growing stronger by the second.

'Mum's book tour of the States lasts another week or so,' he said listlessly. 'Dad might come back a few days early—business, you know.'

I could do with him walking through that door right now, she thought, eyeing the wooden panelled entrance hopefully. On the few occasions she'd met Alan Beck he'd seemed a really warm, friendly person, who'd be quite capable of sorting out his son's problems without any outside help.

'Lucky them. I wouldn't mind being there now.' Being anywhere would be an improvement on here. Soft-hearted? I must be soft-headed!

'Mum doesn't like being away from home.'

With this home who can blame her? Eve thought with a tinge of envy. Next month she'd make herself afford that paint they needed for the kitchen. She didn't actually *need* a new winter jacket; the old one was more than adequate.

'Not like Uncle Drew. *He's* been everywhere.'

Not *Uncle Drew*! Eve's groan was hastily transformed into a soft grunt of interest, which was enough to encourage Daniel to expand eagerly on the theme—she'd known it would be. Her expression glazed over slightly as he warmed to his subject, his pale features becoming animated as he extolled the virtues of his hero.

Eve knew all about Uncle Drew. She could have written a thesis on the man and all the daring, *manly* things he apparently excelled at! Since the uncle had moved in while his parents were away he'd been Daniel's main—no, *only* topic of conversation, with the exception of the predicament this crazy charade was meant to extricate him from.

To Eve, Uncle Drew sounded as if he had a bad case of arrested development. She could easily imagine him as an indulged rich kid growing into just the sort of brash, immature action-man type she couldn't stomach—a prize pain in the posterior!

She gave a small shudder of distaste as she mentally contemplated carefully nurtured biceps and an outsize ego. She strongly suspected half his supposed exploits were very probably fictional. He had to be the world's worst role model for a sensitive type of boy like Daniel, who already had a budding inferiority complex about his lack of sporting ability.

'Uncle Drew says...' Daniel suddenly froze midsentence, and she was spared further worshipful detail.

'They're coming up the drive,' he breathed. His eyes were fixed, horror-struck, on the view through the window of the sweeping drive. 'I can see them! What'll we do?'

'Right, don't panic,' Eve said as her stomach did a nervous back flip. 'Mess up your hair,' she said, regarding him with a critical frown. Ignoring her brother's parting instruction of, 'For God's sake, Evie, show a bit of leg,' she automatically pulled down the black fabric of the short dress she was wearing.

'What?'

'Like this,' she said, rubbing her hands impatiently through the short wavy ebony strands of her own soft, silky cap of hair. 'Here, let me,' she said with ill-concealed exasperation. She leant forward and rumpled the teenager's straggly blond locks. 'Put an arm around me, or something; make it look as if we've been…kissing.'

Daniel made a couple of vague movements towards her. 'I can't. I've never…'

You and me both, mate, she thought, managing a small ironic grin. 'Don't worry, I'll show you what to do.' A classic case of the blind leading the blind!

'I just bet you would, sweetheart.' The deep, cold voice made her start violently. 'But I don't think Daniel requires instruction from the likes of you.' There was the touch of the surgeon's scalpel to the insulting glance that flickered comprehensively over her tall, athletically slender figure.

He summed her up in glance: this was no gauche school-girl; this was a woman who knew what she was doing—and the fact that she planned to do it with his nephew caused Drew Cummings' protective instincts to go into overdrive.

'Likes of me?' Just what the hell did he mean by that? Eve looked indignantly towards the intruder. She didn't have to be particularly intuitive to know that she wouldn't like it, whatever it was!

Even as she was being pulled unceremoniously off the sofa Eve realised she was at last making the acquaintance of the dreadful Uncle Drew. Even if she hadn't, Daniel's faltering, 'I thought you were out,' would have clinched it.

It turned out she'd been wrong to assume Daniel had exaggerated his uncle's physical attributes. The muscles in the arms that were manhandling her were seriously well developed, and the chest she stumbled against was rock-hard—it was also still damp. Uncle Drew had obviously strolled into the room directly from the shower. One towel was looped far too casually for her liking around his slim waist, another was draped over his shoulders. Her sensitive nose quivered as she was treated to a heavy dose of a clean, sharp masculine odour.

'One day you'll be glad I wasn't, Dan.' Drew Cummings flicked a quick, wry grin in his nephew's direction before turning his attention back to Eve. His expression grew openly contemptuous. 'Sorry, sweetheart.' Eyes big and soft as a startled fawn's stared back at him, all confusion and innocence. *Innocence?* That was rich! 'But, unlike Dan, I'm not interested in providing a shoulder for the likes of you.'

A flash of anger flickered into the beautiful dark eyes which had been made even more exotic by skilfully applied make-up. 'Though it didn't look like you were having much luck in that direction from what I saw,' he recalled with a taunting half-smile. 'Besides, it seems to me like you've got more than enough leg to support yourself.' His eyes moved consideringly over her legs, clad in fine denier, as he set her on her own feet.

'Guilt' had to be written in mile-high letters across her forehead she decided drearily, with subtitles of 'scarlet woman' and 'cradle-snatcher' for good measure.

Under the circumstances she was prepared to swallow

his crude insults—just. Even though the snide, sneering superiority of this man made her want to scream. She told herself she had to remember that anyone could and probably would have misread the situation. He was going to feel pretty silly when he knew what was happening, and it was probably time she put him straight. The thought of Drew Cummings feeling silly was a warm thought to cling to when she felt she was drowning in her own humiliation.

'This isn't what it looks like, Mr Cummings.' Calm composure was the best way to defuse this unpleasant situation, she told herself hopefully. *Unpleasant*, Eve? Who are you kidding, girl? This is on par with nightmares of walking around a supermarket stark naked!

'You know my name?' The blue eyes narrowed suspiciously. 'You do your research.'

Name, shoe size, favourite colour... 'Daniel talks about you all the time.'

I bet he does, Drew thought, his eyes slipping of their own volition back to the incredible length of this girl's legs. He'd yet to meet a teenage male who wouldn't tell a female who looked as sleekly sexy as this one just about anything she wanted to know. He could recall all too well what it was like to be ruled by rioting hormones.

She wasn't the type he personally went for, he preferred petite and blonde, but it wasn't hard to see what Dan saw in her. The girl herself obviously had a good nose for money. Call him cynical, but he felt pretty confident about ruling out emotional involvement on her side. One thing was certain: she wasn't getting her hooks any deeper into his nephew.

'That gives you the advantage.' Eve found his smile more threatening than any abuse he might have hurled at her head. 'No, don't tell me your name.'

If Katie ever found out about this he was dead meat. His sister was very protective—over-protective, some might say—of her only child. It had taken all her husband's persuasive powers to convince her that her younger brother was a fit temporary guardian for their son's physical and moral welfare.

'I wasn't going...' Eve began hotly. *Advantage!* If she'd ever been in a situation that had made her feel *less* advantaged she couldn't recall it right now.

The way he'd looked at her—as if she was a piece of meat! She shuddered, and shook her head from side to side as a wave of dizzying fury washed away her last idiotic impulse to apologise. No man had *ever* looked at her like that before.

This musclebound bully wasn't what she'd pictured—he was *worse!* God, but she wished he'd put some clothes on. It was nigh on impossible to avert her eyes from that bare golden-brown flesh; there was so much of it! His shoulders and deeply muscled chest were extraordinarily wide in proportion to his slim hips. Hips that looked far too lean to stop that towel from obeying the laws of gravity. She doubted if the blushes would be his if the unthinkable occurred; modesty wasn't one of the characteristics that leapt to mind when you looked at this man! Now if you were talking insufferable arrogance and smug superiority—*that* was another matter!

Was the hair on man's body normally a shade darker than that on his head? In this man's case a deeper shade of antique gold. The warm, squirmy, unpleasant feeling in the pit of her belly grew unaccountably more intense, and she swiftly raised the level of her eyes—and her thoughts too!

Even in these stupid heels she still had to look up at him, which was a novelty for her, and one she didn't enjoy. He had to be at least six-four or five, she estimated. Concentrating on his face didn't improve her growing sense of antipathy. His angular jaw was hard and uncompromisingly set, and his features, from heavy-lidded startling blue eyes to firm, sculpted mouth, managed miraculously to combine regularity with an individuality which made it impossible to dismiss him as just a pretty face.

If he sneered once more she might just give in to the growing desire to throw an unladylike punch.

'Oh, but you *are* going—and *now*.' The soft observation left no room for negotiation.

'Uncle Drew, don't!' Daniel discovered his voice as his uncle's hand fell heavily on Eve's shoulder. 'You don't understand.'

Some of the implacable hardness died from Drew's eyes as he looked towards his nephew's horrified face. 'I understand, all right. At best she's a tart with a heart, Dan— at worst a predatory little bitch who targets boys like you because anyone with a bit more experience can see past her innocent eyes, beautiful face and sexy body.' It was obvious from the contemptuous curl of his lips as he glanced at Eve which version he favoured.

Sexy body! Eve was so stunned by this assessment that all that emerged from her lips by way of defence was a strangled croak.

'When I came in it looked to me like you were having second thoughts. Am I right, Dan?'

'Yes, But not... She's...' the boy began, throwing Eve a horrified look of apology.

Eve looked at the stuttering boy and willed him to spit out the explanation. Since when did I need people to speak for me? she thought as she was hit by a wave of self-disgust for this display of wimpish behaviour.

'You don't want to learn the stale tricks she can teach you, Dan. Some day you'll understand that fumbling can be a lot of fun, especially when you're both fumbling.'

Eve, taken aback by this unexpected recommendation, caught herself thinking he looked almost human for a second. Was it the memory of a girl he'd fumbled with that brought a quite unexpectedly bleak expression to his eyes? Much more likely it was indigestion, she told herself, dismissing this fanciful notion; he wasn't the type to get mushy and nostalgic about old flames.

The notion of his perfect uncle being personally acquainted with *fumbling* robbed Daniel of his last remaining powers of articulation.

If Nick and his companions, carefully selected for their ability to spread gossip, hadn't entered the room at that moment Eve had no doubts she'd have been ignominiously expelled from the house.

Nick Gordon didn't have to call on his excellent acting ability to display shock. After a brief moment of startled amazement, tinged by a degree of irritation that his excellent plan would have to be ditched, he swiftly assessed the situation and recovered his poise. Damage limitation was the best he could hope for, he decided regretfully.

'Clear out, you lot,' he announced casually.

It didn't occur to Nick that his contemporaries wouldn't follow his instructions. He didn't even glance around to see them leave. Eve found herself envying her sibling's casual ability to inspire obedience.

'What's going on here?'

'Nick, isn't it?' Drew Cummings looked at the tall dark boy with a frown of recognition. 'Did you have anything to do with this little initiation ceremony?'

'You all right, Eve?' Nick said anxiously, ignoring the older man. She looked a bit fraught. Eve took everything so seriously. She really should lighten up, he decided disapprovingly, but he'd never have asked for her help if he'd known it was going to upset her like this.

'Does it look like I'm all right?' *All right?* Eve bit back a hysterical giggle that rose inappropriately to her tight throat. 'Will you sort this out—*now,* Nick?' Her soft, attractive voice rose a quavering octave.

'You know this girl, then?' Drew was looking from brother to sister with hard suspicion. Conspiracy theories began to solidify suspiciously in his head.

'Of course I know her. She's my sister.'

'Do you get your kid brother to pimp for you often, angel?'

A gasp that came from somewhere was loud in the pregnant silence. Eve turned her head and had the brief impression of scalding scorn in those impossibly blue eyes. When Nick's plans went wrong they did so thoroughly, but this present situation was in league of its own.

Let him sort it out. She was out of here. Her first faltering steps turned into a sprint hampered only by the ridiculous heels. She knew her tears were only the irritating outward display of sheer, inarticulate fury, but she wasn't going to let this monster see them and think otherwise.

The door she'd been hammering on for almost the past five minutes finally swung open. Eve watched Theo's expression change from initial lack of recognition to open-mouthed shock.

'Say a word and you're dead,' she promised him venomously, just as the grin was beginning to form. 'I forgot my key.'

The grin was swiftly deleted. 'New look, Evie?' He gave an appreciative leer.

'If we're talking make-overs...?' She allowed her eyes to run speakingly over the tall, rangy figure of her lodger. 'Do the words "ageing hippie" strike a chord?' Head high, slender back ramrod-stiff, she stalked up the stairs trying to ignore the sounds of inexpertly muffled laughter. 'I've had a *very* bad day!' she yelled in warning over her shoulder.

The carpet beneath her feet was beginning to get threadworn. It wasn't the only thing in the big Victorian house that needed replacing—a circumstance that sometimes kept her awake late at night. When her parents had died five years earlier the first thing the solicitors had suggested was putting the rambling old building on the market.

But how could she have wrenched her thirteen-year-old brother away from the only home he'd ever known? He'd already lost his parents, and if they'd moved house he'd have had to change school too. She'd known there wouldn't be enough left after the debts were settled to buy a place in the same area. Their parents had had many admirable qualities, but a knack with money had not been one of them. Eve had been fiercely determined that no matter what happened Nick wouldn't suffer—he'd have all the advantages, bar loving parents, that she had had.

When she'd told the solicitors about her idea they'd regarded her with the sort of superior scorn that some people reserve for teenagers.

Impractical, they'd said. Not economically viable. Well, they'd been wrong, she thought with satisfaction. Five years on and Theo was their only long-term lodger, and, with a few exceptions, they'd been lucky with the succession of people who'd rented the other two rooms in the ugly Victorian monstrosity she'd always called home.

Right now they had a lady librarian in her early thirties and a postgraduate engineering student in his twenties as well as Theo, whom they'd known since they were children. She didn't actually know at what point she and Nick had accepted him as extended family.

Eve had asked Theo once why he stayed, and he'd laughingly told her he was too lazy to move. He'd used to look at property, but he'd stopped pretending some time ago that this was a short-term measure. There had been a few wagging tongues when he'd moved in—she hadn't yet been nineteen and he wasn't exactly in his dotage—but unkind gossip had been the exception even then. Now it was non-existent. Eve thought maybe they—she and the other residents of 6 Acacia Avenue—filled a gap in Theo's life, a gap where, but for a cruel twist of fate, there would have been a wife and children.

The old place ate up the cash, of course, so at the end of the day they weren't much better off financially, but they coped. Actually, she was better off financially at the moment than she'd dared hope, since Nick had won a prestigious scholarship that was going to ease the financial burden of his three years at university considerably.

'Do something reckless with it, Evie,' he'd advised when she'd suggested spending the money she'd been putting aside for his education to replace the leaking flat roof on the kitchen extension.

'*Reckless*,' she said in disgust to her reflection in the mirror on the old mahogany dressing table. She pulled the back of her hand across her crimson-stained lips. This was the last time she let her silver-tongued sibling persuade her to do anything!

'I've planned it with military precision, Evie. Nothing can go wrong.' Nick had played expertly on her soft heart. Soft heart, she thought once again with a disgusted snort—soft brain, more like! Nick's meticulous planning had gone wrong—big time.

She blamed herself for being so easily conned. She should have known things were getting out of hand when Nick had produced the expensive designer outfit belonging to his latest girlfriend's sister and suggested she go into the kitchen to change. She ought to have kicked up a fuss when the girlfriend had produced cosmetics from an apparently bottomless make-up bag. To her amusement the teenager had been scandalised when Eve had casually confessed she didn't actually bother with make-up normally.

In fact, if it hadn't been for a miserable-looking Daniel saying, 'She doesn't have to do it, Nick,' she might well have chickened out there and then. Stripping off the borrowed finery, she wished she had done just that, and been saved the most embarrassing, humiliating experience of her life.

That man, she silently fumed as she tightened the drawstring waist of her loose combat trousers with unwanted viciousness. No wonder poor Daniel didn't confide his personal problems to an insensitive brute like that.

Recalling the flick of those icy cold blue eyes made her feel grubby and guilty all over again. She rubbed fiercely at the rash of goosebumps on her forearms and shuddered. No, she told herself firmly. I refuse to let that feeble excuse for a guardian make me feel like this. I'm not the one who should feel guilty. If Mr Marvellous hadn't been so busy polishing his own ego he might have noticed his charge was suffering a major dose of teenage angst!

Now, of course, she could think of several choice phrases which would have cut that musclebound bully down to size. What had she come up with at the time? 'This isn't what it looks like, Mr Cummings.'

'I still can't believe I said that,' she said out loud.

Theo looked up from the steaming pan to which he was adding indeterminate amounts of a variety of spices.

'Why don't you use the extractor? The whole place reeks of curry.'

'*Curry,*' the tall man repeated with offended dignity. 'That word hardly describes the delicate balance of spices in my work of art.'

'Fine. The whole place reeks of your work of art.' She pulled out one of the mismatched chairs that were set around the long table in the middle of the room and slumped dejectedly down.

'Want to tell Uncle Theo all about it?' he suggested deserting his culinary enterprise with a regretful backward glance.

'About what?'

'Come off it, Evie,' he said bluntly.

She gave a small concessionary shrug and rested her chin upon her arms, which were supported by the comforting solidity of the oak table. 'I've never been so humiliated in my life!' she confided, her voice muffled by the soft fabric of her olive striped top. 'It was Nick's fault.'

'It would be,' her companion acknowledged, speaking with the authority of someone who hadn't escaped un-scathed by that absent young person's inventive schemes. 'You'll feel better if you talk about it.'

Being an innately sensitive human being, he didn't laugh as the whole story spilled out.

'There, I knew it—you think I was stupid!' She lifted her head and tossed a feathery dark curl away from her cheek.

'I think,' he soothed, 'it was a classic case of bad timing.'

'I couldn't refuse, could I?' she appealed to him. 'Poor Daniel was going through hell at school; he's such a sen-sitive boy,' she said, unable to think of his pale, sensitive features without a gush of maternal anguish.

'So it was this girl—the man-eater who came on to him—that spread the rumour in school about him being gay?' Eve nodded. 'But he's not...'

'Gay? Of course not. The poor boy was just petrified by her. Not all seventeen-year-olds are like Nick.' Confidence with the opposite sex was not something that her brother lacked—a fact that had given her several sleepless nights over the last couple of years.

'So Nick was supposed to arrive with an audience guar-anteed to spread the story just as Daniel was in a clinch with the object of all adolescent male fantasies—a desirable mature woman. Overnight his name would be synonymous with stud.'

'In a nutshell…' She pressed her fingers to her temples as if to physically remove the sickening throb of the terrible headache which was developing. 'A case of bad casting, I know.'

'It's quite clever, really,' Theo mused with grudging admiration.

Eve cast her lodger a look of intense dislike. '*Clever!* Pardon me if I don't sound suitably appreciative. I doubt if you would either if you'd been threatened and abused by that disgusting man. Do you know what he called me?' she demanded, her voice quivering with outrage. 'A predatory, grasping little tart who couldn't handle real men.' Even when she closed her eyes she could still see the scornful blaze, hot enough to strip flesh from the bone, in the distinctive blue eyes.

'Ouch.'

'Ouch—is that all you can say?'

'Well, I suppose it must have been a shock for the guy, finding his nephew in the clutches of a—' He came to an abrupt halt and cast her an apologetic lop-sided smile. 'That outfit did make you look pretty—well let's just say you looked the part. Not a tart, you understand,' he added hastily, 'just…'

'You're digging yourself a very deep hole, Theo,' she pointed out, uncharitably glad to see someone other than herself suffering foot-in-the-mouth syndrome. 'He very obviously thought I was a tart.' Her bosom swelled with indignation. 'I suppose *you* think I should be flattered.'

Theo was too wise a man to respond to that challenge. 'Didn't you explain? Didn't the boy put him straight?'

'What chance did I have? I couldn't get a word in edgewise.' Theo looked openly sceptical and she grated her teeth, at a loss to explain to someone who knew her how she'd been inexplicably reduced to a witless zombie by the sheer trauma of the situation. 'Plus the fact,' she continued tartly, 'Nick and his cronies rolled up about thirty seconds after Drew Cummings put in an appearance. It was a circus. And as for Daniel, he obviously thinks the man can walk on water,' she spat in disgust.

When Drew Cummings had entered the room she'd thought for one awful moment his nephew was going to pass out. She'd almost envied him; at the time losing consciousness had had a distinct appeal.

'Talk about macho man!' she added scornfully. 'And I'm positive he's just the type to encourage Daniel's hero-worship. Having a young boy thinking he's a cross between James Bond and Mother Teresa is just the sort of ego stroking he would enjoy. He's the typical product of an over-privileged background—you know the type. He's got that unshakeable sense of his own superiority.'

Theo let out a long, slow whistle. 'And how many products of an over-privileged background do you know on a first-name basis, Evie? You sound as if you're addressing a political rally.'

Eve had the grace to blush. 'You had to be there,' she said defensively.

'This bloke's really got to you, hasn't he? You really shouldn't jump to conclusions, Evie. I thought you were the one down on people who generalised,' he reminded her. 'It's not like you actually know the man.'

The gentle censure in his tone brought a further self-conscious flush to Eve's cheeks. 'True, I don't know him. So things could be worse,' she agreed tartly. Under the circumstances she felt she was being quite restrained.

'God, I wish I had been there—as an observer, of course. Come on, Evie!' he chided. 'This isn't like you. Where's your sense of humour? I don't doubt Nick's sorting things out right now. You'll all laugh about it later.'

Eve stared incredulously at him. Laugh! It was obvious to Eve that Theo failed to appreciate that Drew Cummings was a person totally without redeeming features.

'I hope that *all* doesn't include Uncle Drew. Because I can't conceive of a situation where I'd go within ten miles of the man, let alone share cosy laughter!'

'Talking about Nick—where did he get to?'

'He's big enough to look after himself,' she responded grumpily. All the same, she did glance with some anxiety at the clock. She didn't doubt for a minute that he'd manage to talk his way out of this as easily as he did every other difficult situation he'd ever found himself in his short life— but even so...

'Talk of the devil. That sounds like dear Nicholas now.' At the sound of the front door slamming Theo raised his head from his cooking. 'Follow your nose, Nick, we're in the kitchen,' he yelled. 'Well, well, who's been a— Hellfire, Nick, what happened to you?' Dropping his wooden spoon, an expression of genuine concern on his face, Theo rushed past Eve.

Eve forgot about the cold disdain she'd been going to dish out to her brother and spun around in her seat. With a gasp of horror she too was on her feet.

Nick held out his hands to ward them off. 'It's worse than it looks,' he assured them hastily. The swollen split lip made his voice slightly slurred. 'No, Evie, don't touch... ouch!'

'Ice...' she said firmly.

'Sara's already put ice on it.'

'It looks terrible!' Subconsciously she registered the significant fact that he'd turned to his girlfriend first, rather than her. She saved her contemplation of birds leaving the nest until later—the thoughts uppermost in her mind right now were for Nick's immediate health.

'Thanks.'

'Have you had it checked out in Casualty?'

'Don't fuss, Evie, it's only a bloody nose and a split lip. I'll be my usual beautiful self by next week. Besides, I thought you'd be pleased. Just deserts and all that…' he suggested slyly.

Eve expelled a pent-up breath and relaxed a little now she could see the damage to her brother's face was actually quite superficial. 'If I was a spiteful person…' she only half teased.

'You're mad with me?' Eve grimaced in sympathy as producing his normal winning grin cost Nick a definite wince.

'What do you think?'

'I think you're not ready to see the funny side yet.'

'How intuitive of you. But, first things first, how did you do that?' Her gesture covered the swollen and discoloured area of his mouth and the evidence of a bloody nose.

'It's a bit embarrassing, really,' he admitted, looking sheepish. 'If you'd hung around another thirty seconds you'd have seen for yourself. You know how I always say words are more effective than fists? Well, I've come to the conclusion that that was a very mature statement. Problem is, I wasn't feeling too mature when he…when he said…' He glanced at Theo, his colour heightened slightly. 'That crack about you, Evie,' he finished uncomfortably. 'I just saw red.' The confession was accompanied by a lot of foot-shuffling and shoulder-shrugging. Confessing to the inexplicable urge to protect his sister's honour was obviously affording Nick considerable discomfort.

Eve froze and went dramatically pale. 'Are you telling me,' she said slowly, 'that *he* did this to you?' She recalled the greyhound-lean body and the rippling muscles and a wave of incredulous fury fogged her brain. Nick, for all his height, had the slender body of a young man emerging from adolescence.

'That wouldn't be so embarrassing. The damned man moves incredibly fast for a big bloke,' Nick admitted, his voice tinged with an admiration that was totally incomprehensible to his sister. 'I didn't get to lay a finger on him. I went charging straight past him, tripped over some damn table and straight into some bloody great clock thing. In keeping with the general theme of disaster, it turned out to be an antique family heirloom sort of thing.'

This minor technicality that Uncle Drew hadn't actually laid hands on Nick passed over Eve's head. Her brother was injured, and the damage was directly attributable to Drew Cummings.

'That's it!' Insult her and he might get away with, but cause her baby brother harm and there was no way he was going to escape scot-free!

'What do you think you're doing, Eve?' Her brother asked in alarm as she scrabbled through the small pile of loose keys deposited on the big old-fashioned dresser.

'I'm going to tell Mr Drew Cummings exactly what I think of him, that's what I'm doing. Where are your car keys, Theo?' she continued, ignoring her brother's groan of dismay.

'Don't give them to her, Theo,' Nick pleaded. 'I don't need big sister rushing to the rescue. Tell her, Theo. I just about talked the guy around. The last thing I need is you turning up screaming abuse.'

'I've no intention of screaming, and I'm not doing this for you.' That was true. At least in part. It had really got under her skin that she'd been reduced to some sort of compliant moron earlier. 'I'm doing this for humanity in general. That man needs pulling down a peg or two!' *Why the hell didn't I stand up for myself when I had the chance?* she wondered as she contemplated her missed opportunity with seething frustration.

'I'm not telling her anything.' Eve flashed her brother a

smug grin, which faded as Theo snatched the discovered keys from her hand. 'But neither am I letting you use my car, Evie. Not until you've cooled down.'

'But you know the van's at the garage until tomorrow, Theo,' she wailed reproachfully.

'Then wait until then.'

'How can you say that?' she spluttered indignantly. 'Look at Nick.'

'Nick's already explained the man didn't lay a finger on him.'

'Nick was defending me!' Because I chickened out when the going got tough, she thought with a wave of self-disgust.

'If you're honest, Evie, you're just using this as an excuse because you're itching for a fight.'

'No such thing,' she denied hotly, without meeting his eyes.

'You're mad because you ran away without defending yourself. Or maybe,' he said with an abrupt change of tactics, 'it's a sexual chemistry thing between you and Uncle Drew.' He looked at her with innocent enquiry. 'That could explain all this hostility.' He exchanged a conspiratorial grin with Nick.

'So could being verbally and physically abused,' she replied frigidly. Didn't she have the bruises on her arms to prove it?

'The guy certainly has muscles in all the right places,' Nick agreed solemnly.

'I didn't notice.'

Her brother laughed out loud at this one. 'Maybe you're going back for another look.'

A sharp image of a big bronzed body rose up in her mind to add insult to the injury of her brother's warped humour. A girl didn't go through life without seeing images of male perfection, and Drew Cummings had to fall into that category, but none of those images had assaulted her senses with a raw, earthy sexuality. Of course not. None of them had ever grabbed hold of her whilst half naked, she told herself crossly.

'It's nice to know who your friends are.' She treated them both to her best display of icy dignity as she stalked out of the room.

'I don't think she appreciated the joke,' Nick surmised. 'You don't think she really...?' He looked with comical dismay at the older man beside him. 'Nah,' he said shaking his head.

'Maybe the walk will cool her down?'

'Do you think so?' Nick asked sceptically.

'Not really. I was trying to cheer you up.'

CHAPTER TWO

EVE'S cheeks were tinged pink with exertion after ten minutes of furious pedalling. Serve Nick right if he thought his bike had been stolen. How many times had she told him to chain it up?

Actually, she was forced to acknowledge a definite sense of exhilaration at being the one behaving recklessly for once. It was really quite a liberating feeling, she decided thoughtfully as she ran her fingers through her short, fashionably tousled hair.

She propped Nick's pride and joy against the gleaming paintwork of a big shiny four-wheel drive drawn up on the gravelled forecourt and walked purposefully up to the porticoed entrance. She regarded the pair of stone lions guarding the entrance defiantly.

The door was slightly ajar, and she experienced the first twinge of apprehension as she rang the bell. Her nerves were primed for the offensive, however, and all it took was a quick mental replay of her earlier departure through this very door and the generous lines of her mouth firmed into a line of steely determination and her shoulders squared.

She'd show Uncle Drew she wasn't the sort of girl he could push around, the sort of girl who ran away meekly, the sort of girl who was reduced to inarticulate compliance by a set of bulging biceps and a few harsh words! She liked a joke as much as the next person, but she hadn't found anything humorous in Theo and Nick's appalling suggestions. *Chemistry* indeed!

'Come on through!' A disembodied voice instructed.

Startled, Eve looked over her shoulder, half expecting to find someone these words were directed at standing there.

'Through here!' Impatience this time, and also the distinctive touch of gravel she'd noticed before. A man who didn't suffer fools gladly—or at all.

You heard what the man said, Evie. Don't just stand there, girl. She hadn't expected it to be quite this easy to get back into the Beck residence.

'It's the card table by the door. Can you do it *in situ*, or will you need to take it away? If that's the case I need it back by Thursday at the latest.'

Somehow the top of his dark blond head managed to convey harassment. When his head finally lifted, this impression was reinforced. His hands were still immersed in a bucketful of soapy water as he spoke. 'Well?'

'You don't recognise me, do you?'

'Should I?' he began impatiently, pushing aside a wing of fair hair that had flopped in his eyes. 'You're not the French polisher? Dear God!' he breathed, his eyes widening in recognition. 'It's the *femme fatale*. Not looking very *femme* or *fatale*,' he added unkindly, getting to his feet and rubbing his wet hands against the legs of his jeans.

Eyebrows raised, he let his curious glance run incredulously over her simple stripy top and sleeveless fleece jacket. The loose lines of her khaki pants blurred the outline of her long legs and the flat, practical boots were about as far removed from the strappy stilettos she'd worn earlier as was possible.

It was ironic, considering his initial assessment, that she could now easily be taken for a schoolgirl—and he knew for sure she wasn't. She had a freshly scrubbed, wholesome quality that some men found attractive. Personally, he found the long-limbed athletic look attractive on racehorses rather than women.

Is this display of masculine bad manners meant to make

me feel uncomfortable? Dream on, she thought scornfully. Lips pursed, she deliberately mimicked his action and let her eyes rather obviously wander critically over his body. She didn't actually hold out much hope of finding anything to criticise—she was right.

He was wearing a light-coloured cotton shirt, not tucked into the waist of his jeans. His wet hands had left dark marks on the paler material which outlined thighs that Eve already knew were powerfully muscular. She noticed two wet marks where he'd been kneeling on the floor. He was the sort of man who looked good in any clothes, she reflected, but better without them. Just when her confidence was riding high this random thought sent a flurry of panic zinging along her nerve-endings.

To her surprise, when her flustered glance returned abruptly to his face, she found amused appreciation of her retaliatory action in his expression. A couple of deep breaths and she was able to dismiss her embarrassing observation as an aberration. Stress did things like play havoc with your concentration. She comforted herself with this widely accepted fact.

'What do you want?'

'You can ask that?'

'Oh, you've come to apologise...sorry, I still don't know your name.'

Apologise! Her eyes widened. The cheek of the man! 'I was under the impression that you didn't want to know my name.'

He didn't pretend not to understand her. 'Earlier I was trying to dispel—shall we say, any sense of intimacy.'

Not even a shred of embarrassment, she decided, searching his face. The man was totally shameless. Nick hadn't gone into details—well, actually, honesty forced her to acknowledge she hadn't exactly given him the chance—but this man must know by now she was innocent of sinister intentions towards his nephew.

'Tell me, are you planning to use that?'

'What...? Oh.' She followed the direction of the inclination of his head and flushed deeply as she saw the trowel she was brandishing in her hand. 'I didn't realise...it was in my pocket,' she mumbled in explanation.

'Got anything else muddy and lethal I should know about in there?' he asked, sounding insultingly amused as she shoved the tool back into the capacious pocket of her warm fleece.

'Not muddy.' She took exception to this slur; she was scrupulous about caring for the tools of her trade. 'I'm a gardener—a landscape gardener—freelance.' 'Freelance' sounded more impressive than 'worried about where her next job was coming from'; besides, things weren't really like that any more. Under the circumstances, she had no qualms about making her business sound a lot grander than it was.

After her parents had died she'd had to scale down her plans for the future appropriately. Starting her own garden maintenance business had been a far cry from the degree in landscape architecture she had planned, but what had started as little more than hedge-trimming and lawnmowing had gradually led to better things.

She knew the turning point had been the roof garden she'd created for Adam Sullivan the previous year. He'd been delighted with the results and generous with his praise. And Adam had a lot of upwardly mobile young friends who were keen to employ her services.

'You sound very intense about it,' Drew remarked.

The only evidence of the make-up she'd worn earlier was a slight dark smudging of soft grey kohl around her eyes. Lucky girl. Those eyelashes were a natural ebony that matched her hair. He could think of several women who would kill for those lashes. He took a step closer and noticed the sprinkling of freckles across the bridge of her nose that had been concealed behind a layer of foundation on their last meeting. She had that rarest of all complexions, a genuine peaches and cream one.

'Why shouldn't I be?' she countered, suspecting condescension in his voice. 'Aren't you intense about your work? Is it only the financial wizards in banks who juggle millions who are allowed to take their work seriously?' It was easy to be a big cheese when Daddy Cummings owned the bank, she thought scornfully. How well would he have done if he'd had to fight his way up the ladder?

'My, my, Dan *has* been talking, hasn't he?' Drew mused, mentally adding another subject he needed to bring up with his nephew in the near future. 'But point taken.'

'I'll tell you what I do take seriously, shall I, Mr Cummings?'

His only visible response to her aggressive tone of voice and scornful glare was a quirk of one well-defined brow. 'Feel free, Miss...' What had the boy called her? Just how much of his personal history had Daniel supplied to this young woman? he wondered grimly. He was a man who guarded his privacy zealously, and there were some episodes in his personal history he preferred stayed within the confines of the family.

Well, didn't I make a big impression? He doesn't even remember my name! 'I take people assaulting my brother seriously.'

'Assault! You've got to be kidding, lady! What the hell is your name anyway?'

Eve was pleased to see his air of vaguely amused condescension had vanished. He sounded extremely irritable.

'Eve Gordon.'

'Well, Eve Gordon, I didn't lay a finger on your brother. But if I can't get his blood out of my sister's carpet I might just oblige you.' He gave the bucket at his feet a frustrated kick, and some of the sudsy water splashed on his leather boots.

All he was bothered about was blood on his rotten carpet, when poor Nick might have been scarred for life or bled to death! 'You should have left well alone and got it professionally cleaned.'

Drew, who had just come to this conclusion himself, gave her an unfriendly look. 'I had enough trouble finding a French polisher who'd come straight out and repair the damage your young thug did to the table.'

'I'll tell him you were asking after his health. He'll be so touched by the concern.'

Drew's lips tightened at this dose of irony. 'He looked fine when he left here.'

'I doubt that very much,' she snorted. 'I don't suppose it occurred to you to take him to the hospital. I call it the height of negligence to let an injured boy walk out of here in that state.'

'He didn't walk. A pretty girl picked him up.'

That sounded about right, she grudgingly conceded. Pretty girls were always picking Nick up. Eve suspected pretty girls would be running around after him most of his life. In that respect he probably had quite a lot in common with this man.

'Sara,' she said, not looking mollified by this information.

'If you say so. She was the hysterical type too,' he said dismissively.

'Meaning she couldn't look at the mess you'd made of Nick without displaying some emotion?' She could hardly trust herself to speak at this display of callousness.

'I thought I'd already told you I didn't touch your brother. *I* was the victim of the assault. A fact you appear to be conveniently forgetting. What was I supposed to do? Stand there and let him batter my brains in?'

'One look at you and a person can see straight off how savagely you've been battered,' she observed scornfully, looking at his perfect profile with an expression of disgust.

'Lightning reflexes,' he agreed complacently. 'But come back after my sister sees I've managed to let her house get trashed,' he suggested drily. 'And if she even *suspects* I've allowed her son's morals to be tainted...'

He chose to ignore that Katie's initial response when he'd offered to step into the breach had been to advise him to get a baby of his own if he wanted to play father, or to buy a dog. 'I don't want you practising on mine, Drew,' she'd said frankly.

He still wasn't entirely sure why he'd opted to spend his well-earned holiday here rather than join his friends on the ski-slopes. When Katie had put forward the ridiculous proposition that he was bored he'd laughed, but the more he considered it, the more he was inclined to believe there might well be more than a grain of truth in that accusation.

Eve was unaware that she was chewing her lower lip as she met his taunting look with a belligerently stubborn one of her own. Her blushes were held in check by sheer willpower. 'Not by me.' I probably couldn't taint a moral if I tried, she pondered gloomily—and at twenty-three that was quite an indictment.

Drew shrugged, giving the distinct impression that the minutiae of the incident were of no interest to him. 'Let's just say it'll take more than reflexes to save me then.' He shook the excess moisture off his hands with an expression of distaste. 'When I agreed to keep an eye on Dan I wasn't expecting any of this.'

'Perhaps,' she muttered, 'if you spent more time listening to Daniel and less time talking about yourself, *this* might have been avoided.'

'*Meaning?*'

'I'm sure Daniel makes a very good audience,' she remarked, her eyes opened to their widest and most guileless. 'He *is* very young and easily impressed. We get to hear all about your exploits—second hand, of course, but it brightens up our dull existence no end to hear how the other half live.'

The obvious way to remove that smug, provocative little smile was to... Drew caught himself up short, shocked at the crude, politically incorrect and worryingly tempting solution that had instantly occurred to him. Perhaps a bit of the barbarian lurks in us all, he thought, putting the kiss idea firmly out of his head. He didn't go around kissing strange women—well, not *this* strange anyway!

'You'd know all about bringing up a teenager, I suppose?' It must be at least five minutes since she was one herself.

'If that's meant to be some sort of criticism of Nick...' Eve began hotly. 'I just won't have it!' she declared passionately. 'I'm not saying his idea was a good one,' she conceded reluctantly, 'but his heart's in the right place. He wouldn't have tried to hit you if you hadn't insulted me. I may not be a perfect parent-figure, but I'm proud of Nick, and I won't have some...some male blond bimbo criticise him!'

Drew swallowed the male bimbo crack; he was too astonished at the idea of this woman—hell, she wasn't much more than a girl herself—bringing up a teenager.

'Are you trying to say you're your brother's keeper—in the legal sense?' he asked incredulously.

Eve had come across this response before. There had been a lot of people who had thought that she was ruining her life taking on the responsibilities of a young boy when she was barely eighteen herself. A lot of people who'd urged her to let Social Services take the burden. Opposition had made her all the more determined to keep their family unit intact.

'Until he's eighteen,' she confirmed, her whole stance saying, clearer than words, Want to make something of it? 'Which is next week, as it happens—the same day as Daniel.'

'No wonder you're weird,' he breathed, half to himself. 'I've only been responsible for Dan for weeks, not years, and I'm already feeling ready for the funny farm.'

An unscrupulous tart and now I'm weird—charming! 'It's nice to meet someone who doesn't mince his words,' she observed insincerely. 'As it happens I've found it an extremely rewarding experience watching Nick mature into a warm, caring young man.' Her lovely mouth curved into a faintly disdainful bow as she selectively deleted all the low points—and there had been quite a few during the last five years. 'A wise man knows his limitations, and there's nothing wrong at all with being self-centred. I'm sure you're extremely wise to avoid responsibilities.'

Neck extended, he allowed his head to roll back in a relaxed, sleepy way. Eve began to think her provocative words had been too subtle for the pea brain to take in— until she saw the steely expression in his half-closed eyes as he looked down at her. Maybe not that subtle, she conceded, swallowing hard—maybe not subtle enough, a small, cowardly voice suggested.

'Wisdom.' He considered the word slowly as it rolled thoughtfully off his tongue.

It gave Eve time to give his mouth a detailed examination. Unlike her own, it was perfectly proportioned. She came to the conclusion that there was something quite cruel about the thin upper lip, and there was a disturbing sensuality to the full lower curve. An unexpected tingle of excitement bubbled through her veins and her heart-rate picked up tempo in response. Stimulating? Exchanging insults with this man? Next thing she knew she'd be playing on the railway track. There wasn't much to choose between the two pursuits.

'Is that the same sort of wisdom you displayed when you decided to play the sultry temptress? A snogging session on the sofa with a schoolboy?' He awaited her reply with an expression of rapt interest. 'I suppose it's possible,' he prompted, 'that you like 'em young. Some women do. Or were you living out your naughty fantasies? Then again I might be barking up the wrong tree completely. Do your tastes run in an entirely opposite direction?' He looked thoughtfully at her sensible shoes.

Her cheeks went bright red as she caught the drift of his crude insinuations. 'I was not…not…'

'Snogging?' he prompted her helpfully.

'It's not men I don't like. Just you!' The nostrils of her masterful little nose flared and she looked at him with loathing. 'As for kissing… I didn't… I wouldn't!' she spluttered furiously.

'I thought it was Dan who wouldn't.' The breath escaped from between her clenched teeth in a noisy gasp. His smile was a gentle pat on the head. 'Probably afraid of being eaten alive. That was some outfit.' And some body that had filled it out, he added mentally—though you'd never suspect it right now. Talk about camouflage! 'Don't take the rejection too much to heart. Your average *adolescent* would have leapt at the chance—and leapt at you too,' he added thoughtfully.

'Meaning a proper man would have had more sense?'

'Sensitive nerve?' he suggested with a maliciously sympathetic smile. 'Sorry.'

'You know where you can stick your apology!' she hissed.

'I can imagine,' he responded hurriedly. 'But don't get anatomical, I beg you; I have a very delicate stomach.'

Delicate! she silently raged. Do me a favour—he's about as sensitive as a brick!

'Poor Dan has been going through hell at school,' she told him passionately. She was too angry to notice the spasm of self-recrimination that tautened her opponent's handsome features momentarily. 'Kids can be incredibly cruel.'

Did she think he needed telling? he wondered. The fact the kid hadn't told him bit deep—he hadn't noticed any of the clues, and, in hindsight, those clues had been glaringly obvious. He'd been a miserable failure as a guardian.

'Can't you remember what it was like to be singled out as different?' Eve's dark eyes swept disparagingly over him, from the tip of his blond head to his expensively shod feet, and she realised she was looking at the boy everyone else had wanted to be, not a loner isolated by quirks of nature. 'No, I don't suppose *you* can. I was only trying to help.'

'Save me from fool women with good intentions!' She'd obviously approve of him more if he could produce evidence of childhood trauma. 'Alas, I can't wheel out a dysfunctional family, even though I can see the fact my parents are kind, loving, well-balanced…and, yes, well-off individuals ruins my credibility in your eyes.'

'They must be wondering where they went wrong with you.'

'You really can't stop with the cheap wisecracks, can you? Dear God, I wouldn't give you custody of my cat, let alone a child! Didn't it occur to you to tell me before you embarked on your crazy scheme?'

'It wasn't my…' she began. She closed her mouth. She wasn't about to lay the blame at her brother's door. After all, she had been a co-conspirator and the allegedly responsible adult; she *should* have known better. It was hav-

ing this awful man point out the fact—very unpleasantly—
she couldn't stand.

'Dan made us swear not to. He didn't want his fantastic
Uncle Drew to think he was a wimp. Tell me, what does
it feel like to be a role model?'

A dull red ran up under Drew's perfect tan. Her smile
of triumph faded and a soundless squeak escaped her lips
as she realised with horror she was wondering how far that
golden colour extended. She hadn't seen any demarcation
lines earlier.

'So you decided you were better qualified to deal with
this problem than, say, his parents, or guardian, or head-
teacher? Isn't there anyone who can put the brake on your
wild ideas? What did your partner think of the scheme? Or
didn't you tell him? I take it he *is* a he?'

Eve knew in that second she'd die rather than admit her
unattached state. Up until this point she hadn't attached a
stigma to her single state, but under the mocking glare of
those hateful, knowing eyes things looked very different.

'Very much so. Theo is very supportive of anything I
do.' It sounded so smooth she was quite impressed herself.

Please forgive me, Theo, she thought, hoping she didn't
look as guilty as she felt. He wouldn't mind her using his
name in a good cause, she told herself. Question was,
would he think scoring points off Drew Cummings a good
cause?

'Meaning you walk all over him in your hobnailed
boots.' He lifted a supercilious eyebrow as he gazed at the
footwear. 'Poor guy.'

'He doesn't need your sympathy!' She ground her even
white teeth silently.

'No, he needs therapy.' He looked pointedly at her
clenched fists and shook his head. 'A family trait, I see.
There was some point was there, to you barging in here,
Miss Gordon?'

Good question, Eve. What *are* you doing here? Other than coming second in this battle of words, that is.

'I did not barge in; I was invited.' Pity Nick *hadn't* landed him a punch, she thought wistfully.

'I won't make that mistake twice,' he assured her.

'I *was* hoping you'd display some remorse for causing Nick's injuries and for treating me so appallingly. We all know your hands and feet are lethal weapons. You didn't need to beat up on a teenager to prove it.'

'Past tense, I see…you've decided my character's as black as your hair, I suppose?'

On impulse he flicked the feathery end of one ebony curl that lay against her temple. There was a definite blue sheen to her hair when the weak winter light caught it. Against his fingers the texture was just as silky as it appeared. Eve leapt back as if he'd struck her.

'Don't touch me!' she breathed, shaking her head to dispel the warm, muzzy sensation that filled her brain. The messages whizzing around in her head seemed to be having trouble connecting.

Drew Cummings held up his hands in mock surrender. 'Sounds like the best advice I've had all day.' He didn't go in for spontaneous physical contact with strangers, and he felt annoyed with himself for doing so now. 'Tell me, do you always act like something out of a Victorian melodrama? It must get exhausting living with you.'

Eve chewed down hard on her full underlip, well aware that her instinctive response had been way over the top. 'I think it's perfectly legitimate for me to be nervous after you manhandled me earlier.'

'I was as gentle as a lamb. Remarkably restrained, actually.'

'*Really?*' she said scornfully. She lifted both hands and let the sleeves of her thin top fall back. 'Pardon my scepticism.' The faint blue discoloration made by his fingertips showed clearly on the pale skin of her wrists.

His vivid blue eyes deepened abruptly to navy blue, and a deep line appeared between his brows. 'I didn't do that.' His voice held an edge of revulsion.

The impact her display had made surprised Eve. She'd expected some slick, sarcastic retort. 'No? Let your mind slip back a few hours. You were hauling me about like a sack of coal.'

'God, I'm really sorry. I had no idea.' He reached out and firmly took her hands. Eve searched his face curiously and saw only genuine concern. This wasn't just a line he was shooting her, she realised. He really was sorry. 'Dear God, you must be fragile. I can only say it was unintentional.'

Her slim build hid a wiry strength, not on a par with his, but nonetheless she was no delicate flower. Eve didn't point this out. The constriction in her throat made it hard to point anything out.

This time she didn't recoil. That strange slow motion thing was happening again, and she didn't have the will or desire to fight it. She let herself go with the flow. Drew turned her arm slowly over and back again, examining the blue-veined inner aspect of her forearm. His own hands were nicely shaped—big, capable hands, with long, tapering fingers.

'There's no need to make a fuss about it,' she began, trying to put some emphasis into her husky-sounding voice. She could see the fine lines which time would etch deeper radiating from the corners of his eyes. Letting her flickering, wary gaze dwell on the deep azure warmth of his eyes made her feel dizzy. On the whole she had felt a lot better when those eyes had been ice chips. A man holding your hand should have no effect whatsoever on the stability of your knees, she told herself sternly—it made no sense at all.

He'd had enough time to make a map of the area by now! The soft contact was incredibly abrasive to her vulnerable nerve-endings. Nobody would have guessed from the activity of her heart that she was in the peak of physical condition. This wayward organ was pumping at a rate of knots, and her breath was coming in short breathy gasps.

What did he think he was doing anyhow? Running fingers that had never seen an honest day's work in their lives over her skin. Eve had had some very uncomfortable interviews with bankers in her time. More important, what was she doing letting him?

'It's nothing...I bruise easily. I only told you to make you feel guilty.' She didn't add that she hadn't expected to succeed.

'You smell...' His voice was kind of distracted, and when he lifted his head from his prolonged contemplation of his handiwork she saw his blue eyes were still burning with a very worrying light. Eve thought it wise not to dwell too long on those hot, hungry eyes.

'I'm sorry my personal hygiene doesn't meet with your approval.' She dredged around and from somewhere managed to find sarcasm.

'Nice,' he growled. 'You smell nice. I don't recognise the perfume.' Without actually touching her he inclined his head to breathe in the fragrance of her hair. The sudden compulsion bothered him—annoyed him. And it showed in the downturn of his lips.

'It's soap. Probably the medicated one I bought for Nick's acne,' she elaborated prosaically. Flat-out panic felt like a heartbeat away. Had someone turned up the thermostat in the room? She couldn't breathe properly.

'Acne,' Drew echoed flatly. His thumb had moved to the

delicate hollow of one elbow; the circular motion sent a tingling down to her curling toes.

'Teenage complaint from which you were no doubt immune.' This person was invading her body space. She ought to be sending out some clear and unambiguous signals that read 'Get off!' loud and clear. Instead, what was she doing? Probably acting like every other female this man had ever touched—a compliant push-over.

'It isn't a subject that springs immediately to mind when I'm responding, albeit reluctantly, to a mutual chemical attraction.'

Not him too! Chemical…chemistry…they'd all gone stark staring bonkers. Her eyes narrowed. She hadn't missed the 'reluctant' bit either. Aren't I up to his usual standard? she wondered truculently.

'I'd worry about the chemical reaction going on under your feet if I were you.'

He cursed with satisfying distress as he followed the direction of her gaze.

'I told you, you should have got a professional cleaner,' she reminded him cheerfully as she rubbed her toe against the newly bleached area underfoot. Things had got a bit silly, but she was in control again now, she decided with a relieved sigh.

He lifted his head and caught the tail-end of her surreptitious grin. 'Maybe you won't be laughing so much when I send you the bill?'

Eve hoped this was an empty threat, because her tight budget wasn't up to surprises like that. 'Does this mean you don't love me after all?' she pouted, giving a passable impression of a spurned lover. He was obviously one of those men who tried it on with any female that had a pulse, she thought with disgust.

Actually, she'd never been spurned; she'd done a bit of minor spurning herself—there had been that lovely Adam with the roof garden who'd wanted to get closer, and one or two others, but none had lit any answering spark in her.

Sparks! She glanced gloomily at her feet and had a sharp mental image of flames curling over the practical footwear she wore. 'Sparks' didn't begin to cover the conflagration she'd been recklessly flirting with. It was all some nasty hormonal conspiracy; an example of the weakness of the flesh from which she'd learn a valuable lesson once she was safely home and away from this man. She might even be able to decide what the lesson was then.

'It's possible I might be able to give you up without aversion therapy.'

'I'll try to be stoical about it,' she promised evenly. Didn't aversion therapy involve repeated exposure to the thing you wanted to give up? Now there was a very unsettling thought!

'I'll always cherish our time together.'

Sarcastic pig! 'How fortunate you are to possess a shallow and superficial nature,' she said sunnily. She suddenly wished she was still wearing the feminine armoury of earlier. For some reason she felt it would have made it a lot easier to smile in the face of this masterly put-down if she'd known she looked feminine and...well...sexy. 'For an awful moment I thought I might have to fight off your advances,' she confessed.

His white even teeth clamped together in a snarl-like smile. 'If those are the signals you send out when the options you're considering are fight or flight you could have serious problems,' he told her drily.

'I hope you're not suggesting I wanted you to kiss me!' she yelled. The smug smile made her want to stamp her feet in childish frustration. 'You're delusional, and even more in love with yourself than I thought!'

Head on one side, he observed her pink cheeks and heaving bosom thoughtfully. 'Are you trying to goad me into kissing you?'

Her mouth opened and closed soundlessly several times. 'Are you...*mad*?' she squeaked hoarsely.

'I'm not going to kiss you into submission, you know,' he informed her apologetically. 'Don't get me wrong—I can see the appeal. If only,' he observed, half to himself, 'to get you to shut up. You're just not really my type.'

'You're pathetic,' she grated incredulously. 'Do you actually think that every female you meet fantasises about being swept up in your strong arms?'

'This is what I was worried about,' he said sadly. 'You just want more than I can give. I wanted to save you this hurt and humiliation.'

Now she knew for sure he was winding her up, having a good laugh at her expense. He must have noticed she'd been shaking feverishly when he'd taken her hand. He obviously found the whole idea of her finding him attractive hilarious.

'You're very considerate.' She'd had enough of being the live entertainment. It really went against the grain to retreat, but she could do it with dignity at least. 'I'm going home now. I hope for Daniel's sake his parents aren't going to be away much longer.'

He smiled wryly. He'd instinctively known she was the sort of female who had to have the last word. Drew listened for the inevitable crash of the front door before he sat down in one of the luxuriously upholstered chairs. He couldn't help wondering what it would have been like if he'd actually kissed that strident, volatile young woman.

The entrance of his nephew halted the erotic nature of his thoughts.

'Have a seat, Dan. I think we need to talk.'

'Again?'

'Again. Now, just what exactly have you told Nick and his peculiar relations about me?'

'Not much.'

'And does that ''not much'' include the Lottie saga?'

'No! I wouldn't tell *anyone* about that, Uncle Drew.'

CHAPTER THREE

A BLAST of warm air hit Eve as she entered the scullery. She was physically tired, but happy. At times like this she was conscious of how few people enjoyed their work as much as she did, and she felt very fortunate as the weary glow of well-being enfolded her.

To her surprise a somewhat breathless daughter of the house appeared in the doorway so swiftly it was obvious she must have been hovering close by. Her face fell ludicrously when she saw Eve.

'Oh, I thought…I thought you were someone else.' The glossy blonde hair surrounding her flower-like face swung like a silky bell as she shook her head self-consciously.

Someone important enough to make this beautiful, sophisticated woman behave like a breathless teenager must be quite someone, Eve reflected as she rubbed her frozen fingertips together. They began to tingle as her sluggish circulation hotted up.

'Your mother asked me to stop by for a cup of tea when I'd finished, Mrs Hall,' Eve explained apologetically. Beyond the adjoining door to the kitchen she could hear sounds of activity.

'I did indeed.' Mrs Atkinson, dressed with impeccable elegance in a soft grey crêpe two-piece, entered the room behind her daughter. 'Take a seat, Eve, my dear. You know Charlotte, don't you.'

Eve nodded politely. As she hadn't been invited into the kitchen she didn't bother removing her boots. She'd been briefly introduced to the elegant woman when Charlotte had arrived from the airport the previous evening, her slender body encased in a floor-length silver fur coat almost exactly the same shade as her hair.

Eve had exchanged the customary pleasantries and departed inclined to give the other woman the benefit of the doubt where the fur was concerned; it probably wasn't real. Eve had been left with an impression of style, gloss and cut-glass beauty. She doubted if she'd left any impression at all on the other woman.

Right now Charlotte Hall seemed on edge and brittle, but the edge of vulnerability didn't detract from her fragile, classically perfect beauty.

'Mummy tells me you've been restoring the knot garden. It must be a bit cold at the moment to be working outdoors.' She glanced out of the window at the frost-covered garden and shuddered.

She reminded Eve of a delicate hothouse orchid that would shrivel in the Arctic conditions that were sweeping the country, making this the coldest January in living memory.

'Charlotte's been living in California; she's forgotten what a proper winter is like. Don't you fret. Eve here is very sturdy, but actually she's been doing some work in the greenhouses for us today.'

Eve tried and failed to look on 'sturdy' as a compliment. Compared with the diminutive creature dressed entirely in black, which did marvellous things for her translucent complexion, she felt like an ungainly giant.

'California. That sounds exciting. Will you be visiting for long?' Eve asked, receiving her steaming mug with a smile of thanks.

Charlotte glanced at her mother quickly and lowered her eyes, a mysterious smile playing about her lovely lips. 'Possibly,' she said enigmatically. 'Will you excuse...?' She drifted ethereally from the room.

'She's a bit on edge,' Mrs Atkinson confided. 'I've arranged a little luncheon party.'

'I was just going,' Eve said, taking the hint.

'No, there's no need for you to hurry.'

Eve settled back down, even though her schedule was tight. Mrs Atkinson was a woman with a lot of time on her hands, who liked to chat, and Eve, a good listener, usually obliged.

'Actually, it's rather awkward. Charlotte used to be engaged to the young man we're expecting. It was a couple of years ago now, but she's not actually seen him since…well, actually…she walked out at the last minute, just before the wedding.'

'You mean she jilted him?' Eve gasped, goggle-eyed. 'I mean, I'm sure she had her reasons,' she added hastily as she saw the maternal hackles visibly rise.

Mrs Atkinson looked mollified. 'Actually…' She gave a rueful sigh. 'She didn't actually tell us why, but everyone knew it must have been something very bad to make her act so out of character. They'd been a couple on and off since schooldays, you see—inseparable. She ran off to America and married Rufus Hall eventually; he's very rich, of course,' she added.

Eve wondered whether this was some sort of justification. Had the old boyfriend been struggling and poor? Eve felt her romantic side warm to the idea, seeing in her mind this poor unfortunate as impecunious, but sensitive. She found herself hoping he'd found true love elsewhere, and wouldn't need the fickle affections of Charlotte Hall.

Expensive perfume wafted over Eve as Mrs Atkinson bent forward. 'There's to be a divorce,' she hissed. 'Her father and I are devastated.'

Eve didn't quite know how to respond to these confidences. 'Very sad,' she said neutrally.

Was this a case of off with the old, on with the older?

Was Charlotte trying to get back together with her ex-flame? Considering the way she'd rushed into the room when she'd heard the door open it seemed she was very anxious to see her old boyfriend. She must be pretty sure of her own irresistibility if she thought he'd be willing to overlook being left standing at the altar.

'Of course we'd be delighted if she decided to move back to this country. Perhaps it's selfish, but she's our only child.' She looked thoughtful. 'It would be perfect if she and....' She shook her head and smiled, apparently aware she was on the verge of being indiscreet. 'But I mustn't ramble on, my dear.'

Eve accepted her cue and got to her feet. 'Thanks for the tea. I'll see you next week,' she said briskly. 'And I hope your lunch goes well.'

'What a sweet girl you are.'

The four-wheeled drive had just pulled up on the driveway as Eve reached her van. 'Blast and damnation,' the *sweet girl* muttered as she saw the driver had effectively blocked her in.

At least, she reflected with a guilty grin as she walked over to the driver's side of the other vehicle, I'll be able to satisfy my curiosity and see what the old flame looks like. Compared to me, people do seem to lead very dramatic lives, she thought with a grin.

'Sorry,' she said leaning forward to a window which swished silently open as she approached. 'Could you back up a little? I can't get out. Good God!' she ejaculated as the driver's face came into view. '*You're* the one she jilted!' Strike 'impecunious' and 'sensitive'!

'It is my one claim to fame,' Drew Cummings agreed drily. Could it be someone had set up an Internet page devoted entirely to his disastrous love-life? He resolved to have a long talk to Dan that would revolve around the general theme of loose tongues costing lives—in this case his nephew's!

Close to, he could see the frosty wind had turned the tip of Eve's nose pink, and the rest of her face glowed healthily. During her stroll over to his car he'd been able to take in the full glory of her fantastic legs, clad today in faded and quite snug-fitting jeans.

Eve's eyes became saucer-like with horror at the words which had leapt from her unruly tongue. 'Oh! I'm so sorry. I didn't mean to just blurt it out like that, honestly. It was just seeing you, of all people...' She stopped and grimaced, aware she wasn't making matters much better. 'It's none of my business.' Uncle Drew a jilted lover! He was the very last man in the world she would have imagined being left at the altar.

'True, but I've noticed that doesn't stop you butting in. Don't apologise. I can see I've made your day, and I do like to spread a little joy. Most people manage to disguise the worst of their prurient curiosity—but, hell, you go right ahead and enjoy yourself.' Drew slid out of the vehicle and slammed the door in a controlled sort of way.

'Under no circumstances would I call talking to you enjoyable,' she countered tartly, forgetting for the moment she was talking to an object of pity.

It occurred to her as she took in the casual elegance of his loose-fitting Italian suit and open-necked jersey shirt that he and Charlotte Hall must have made a stunning couple. Individually they were both head-turners; together they must have inspired universal envy.

'You took me by surprise,' she accused.

'Sorry,' he remarked, in an ironic tone that made her flush.

'I wouldn't normally be so cruel or unkind.'

'You thought for me you'd make an exception? I'm touched.'

'I don't take pleasure from other people's misfortunes,' she added loftily.

'What, not even a little?' he mocked, judging the distance between his thumb and forefinger through narrowed eyes. She shook her head angrily and he laughed. 'Well, you must be a very unusual person, Eve Gordon, because for most people something as juicy as a jilted bridegroom brings on a nice warm glow.'

'Wallowing in self-pity does the same for other people.' She winced, and looked up at him with genuine remorse. 'That was an awful thing to say,' she said impulsively. 'I'm really sorry. It's a terrible thing to happen—to anyone. I expect you got over it a long time ago,' she added comfortingly. 'You wouldn't be here if you hadn't.' I'm babbling, she thought, trying desperately to bring her tongue to heel before she really said something awful—*more* awful, she mentally corrected.

'Would it make you feel even worse if I said there are some things a man *never* gets over?' he enquired with interest as he watched with malicious amusement Eve getting tied in knots in her attempts to soothe his injured feelings. Despite the fleeting display of pity, which he loathed, he found he was enjoying himself.

Eve looked at him suspiciously as he struck a dramatic pose, one hand pressed to the region where his heart *ought* to dwell. Was this a case of double bluff? she wondered. Was the flippancy to cover the extent of his real feelings? Admittedly he didn't look like a man deeply traumatised, but you never could tell—Theo didn't act like a man with a broken heart either. Expelling her breath in a gust of warm air that grew instantaneously frosty white, she made a conscious decision to stop trying to redeem herself.

'Well, in that case you'll probably be very happy she's getting divorced.'

Drew shot her a very hard look, the mocking light dying

from his eyes. 'Lottie?' he snapped, his dark brows drawing together in a straight line.

Lottie—Charlotte, they must be the same person. Eve was startled. She'd sort of assumed he knew more about the situation than she did.

'Didn't you know? Isn't that why you're here?'

'I'm here for lunch with old family friends. More to the point, how do *you* know?'

'Well, she didn't tell me, but her mother...'

'Are you telling me Lottie is here—*now*?' he demanded. Self-discipline couldn't prevent the colour seeping dramatically from his face.

Suddenly he wasn't so cool and confident. Eve ought to have felt pleased, in a spiteful, mean-minded sort of way, that she'd inadvertently punctured his egotistical bubble. Inexplicably this display of vulnerability didn't make her feel any happier. If anything her mood became blacker.

'Waiting to enfold you in a loving embrace,' she informed him sourly. Some women didn't know when they'd had a lucky escape. 'Before you ask, she didn't say that either. But I did gain the distinct impression that it's kiss and make-up time. Face it, you've been set up.'

'Hell!' he cursed, flickering a quick look towards the charming timbered façade of the old Tudor manor house. He touched her shoulder lightly, his blue eyes searching her face. 'This isn't a wind-up?'

She shook her head indignantly. 'Why would I...?'

'All right, all right...' He hushed her indignant objections in a slightly distracted, irritated way. 'Be quiet, will you, woman? I'm thinking!' he ordered peremptorily. His steely gaze swept beyond Eve's ostentatious display of anger.

She sarcastically clicked her heels and brought her hand up in a smart salute. When he still ignored her she stamped her feet on the frosty ground and blew on her cold fingertips. What a time to forget her gloves. It hadn't got above freezing all day. Did he think she had nothing better to do than wait around here for him to eventually get around to moving his damned car?

'Listen, I want you to do something for me.'

'No, I want *you* to do something for *me*. Move your car so I can leave, remember?' What was it with this man? Did he think her life revolved about him?

'I want you not to scream or yell.'

She cast a suspicious frown up at him. 'Why would I…?'

'On second thoughts, make that total silence.'

Eve didn't have time for first, second or any other thoughts as she was being kissed on her slightly parted lips. She didn't scream or yell, but she did kick him very hard in the shins—eventually. This hadn't been strictly necessary to call a halt; it wasn't as if he'd had hold of her or anything. He'd just bent forward and almost casually placed his mouth against her own.

When he did draw back she was panting for air like a stranded fish. The healthy glow had faded from her cheeks, leaving her pale with anger. Her glittering sloe-dark eyes rested contemptuously on his face. She found them sliding automatically to his lips.

'Eventually' had left far too much time to appreciate the firm texture of that sensual mouth. Not that she'd appreciated it as such; the slow, sensuous movement had been calculatingly callous. It had been a cynical display of expertise designed to reduce his victim to trembling compliance. She firmly pushed aside the memory of the searing contact.

'Excellent,' he murmured as the roar of blood was receding in her ears. 'What a pal you are, Eve. Consider the bill for the carpet ripped up,' he added magnanimously.

Pal? Talk about adding insult to injury! Pals, at least hers, didn't go in for mouth-to-mouth contact; they contented themselves with a handshake or an affectionate hug. Eve would *never* be throwing her hugs in his direction!

'Don't worry, she's gone,' he told her, rubbing his bruised shin against his uninjured calf. 'Lottie was watching us from the window,' he explained, as comprehension didn't dawn on Eve's pale features.

Eve might have got it wrong. In fact Drew thought she had. It would have been bizarre if Lottie had been expecting him to walk in and act as if nothing had changed over the past two years. On the other hand, why hadn't the Atkinsons told him she was going to be here? The fact they hadn't did suggest this might be a set-up.

To be on the safe side, the kiss had been a calculated exhibition of reality. If she did have any unrealistic expectations, Lottie needed to know he *could* kiss other women now. His glance returned to the outline of Eve's full lips. And enjoy it—enjoy it a lot.

She might be screaming foul now, but Eve had definitely responded. The ache in his loins was still a flagrant, distracting reminder of the memory of her soft, yielding body plastered against him.

He'd imagined meeting Lottie again so many times, and now it was here all he could think about was that tiny throaty gasp as his tongue had thrust into Eve's mouth.

Indignation made her feel dizzy. It had to have been something like that, of course. Eve wasn't stupid enough to imagine that display had been for her benefit.

'Going to make her suffer before you crawl back, are you, Uncle Drew?'

Charlotte Hall née Atkinson was the woman he'd thought of when nostalgically recalling mutual fumbling; Eve was sure of it. If he didn't still care he wouldn't have needed to stage that little performance. His first love, maybe his last? Two twin flags of colour appeared on the crest of her

sharply curving Slavic cheekbones as these uncomfortable
conclusions chased each other through her head.

'At one time I lulled myself to sleep with sweet dreams
of flaunting my lovers under Lottie's nose,' he admitted
frankly. 'She was going to wake up to what she'd been
missing.' He seemed amused rather than bitter at this wry
recollection. 'Actually, I find the possibility of being in a
position to do the rejecting embarrassing. What did you call
me?' he added abruptly.

Eve didn't bother hiding her scepticism. 'Talk about pathetic,' she continued in a disgusted voice. 'Even for the
spur of the moment that wasn't a very original thing to do.
Do you think kissing *me*'s going to convince her you
haven't been pining away?'

'You do yourself an injustice, Eve,' he said in a soft,
suggestive voice that made the fine hair on her nape quiver.
'And I hate to destroy your illusions, but I haven't kept
myself pure and chaste since Lottie left me. Despite what
my sister says, neither have I slept with a different female
every night.' His expression was hard and cynical.

In Katie's opinion, which she voiced loudly and often,
he was over-compensating for being a one-girl man for so
long—either that or having his revenge on the entire female
race by breaking as many hearts as possible. But his morals
and his sexual appetite actually weren't nearly as shocking
as his sister imagined, and he'd always parted company
with his female companions amicably. He was very careful
only to get involved with women who could handle relationships that didn't follow the traditional path to commitment, marriage and babies.

Katie had warned him he wouldn't be satisfied with this
frivolous, selfish lifestyle for ever, but he had every intention of proving her wrong. When you'd been once bitten
the way he had you made damned sure that number two
never even appeared on the distant horizon.

'I'll sleep better knowing that,' Eve responded faintly. You just didn't go around talking to virtual strangers like this. She didn't think she was being particularly gauche to feel distinctly uneasy and out of her depth with the direction this conversation was taking. She'd better do some redirecting quick-smart.

'I think balance is important in all things, including sex. And I'm talking sex here…'

'I wish you wouldn't,' she breathed.

'Not sentimental love,' he clarified, despite her plea for ignorance. His voice carried a deeply scornful inflection that made it quite clear he didn't think much about romantic love these days. 'I don't let my libido rule me, but I do enjoy myself.'

'How sad,' she responded impetuously.

'Sad?' he echoed sharply.

'Fast cars, high-powered job, trophy girlfriends—it sounds like a male teenager's fantasy, but for a grown man it just seems a bit empty and, well…sad to me,' she confessed.

His deep blue eyes widened. She didn't even sound judgemental; incredible as it was, the little wretch had the cheek to feel sorry for him! The novel experience of being an object of pity went severely against the grain.

'I suppose your life is deeply fulfilling?' he returned in a clipped, unamused tone.

'Sorry, I should have kept my opinions to myself.' She gave an understanding nod. 'You don't like pity; neither do I. Was Charlotte your first…? Oh, no, I shouldn't have said that!'

What a nice, impersonal sort of question, Eve, she told herself, biting her impetuous tongue so viciously she could taste the salty tang of blood. Her cheeks felt hot enough to melt most of the ice in the vicinity. You just didn't go around asking a man when and with whom he'd lost his virginity!

Drew was accustomed to being around females whose conversation was as beautifully manicured as their nails. After the initial shock had worn off he was finding this girl's painful forthrightness quite refreshing—stimulating, even.

'Lottie and I started dating when we were still at school.' His beautifully shaped mouth quivered ever so slightly, but his expression remained grave. 'Shall I elaborate…?' He repressed a grin. From her expression, she wasn't so keen to be on the receiving end of candour.

'No! Please…that's not necessary. I think it's very… very…'

'Nauseating?' he suggested with a thin smile. 'Please,' he begged urgently, 'don't say *sweet*.'

'Well, it is. I think it's a pity you've let the experience turn you cynical and jaundiced.'

'You sound like my sister.'

'The brother I've got is more than enough,' she assured him crisply.

'I thought bringing him up had been a deeply rewarding experience.'

'It is sometimes, and other times,' she said with a rush of frankness, 'it's frustrating, worrying and exhausting! I don't think I have influenced Nick's development very much,' she mused. 'He has a *very* strong personality and he's always been incredibly self-sufficient.'

'The ''strong personality'' part appears to be a genetic trait you share.'

'Do you feel threatened by strong women?' she challenged, reading criticism in his observation. 'Bossy' was an adjective that had been inaccurately applied to her more than once. Her best friend Alice had frequently told her she scared men off.

'No, attracted,' he announced frankly, with no discernible change of expression. 'I've an allergy to clinging.' His lips moved in a moue of distaste.

Her capable, self-reliant, independent Woman of the Millennium pose vanished without a trace in the face of this breath-stealing announcement.

'Are you flirting with me?' she demanded. She was aware she didn't sound as outraged as she ought. At least she'd managed to avoid purring encouragement; that was a small mercy.

'I don't think I'm brave enough. Besides, there's always the boyfriend.' His blue eyes narrowed slightly, and Eve wished she was more accustomed to carrying off a lie convincingly. Her guilt felt out of proportion to the convenient fib. 'I'm beginning to wonder about the boyfriend,' he said slowly, confirming all her worst fears. 'It seems to me for someone handing out lessons you don't know much about kissing, do you, Eve?'

Not content with humiliating and insulting her, he was now telling her she was a rotten kisser! She wanted to yell, 'What would you know?' But common sense prevented her; it had been painfully obvious he knew quite a lot!

'Unlike you, I don't consider kissing to be an intellectual exercise. I can't divorce my mouth from my emotions.'

'I'd noticed that.' His eyes rested on her lips with an expression that made her stomach muscles clench quite suddenly. 'The other day I nearly kissed you—let's be honest, you wanted me to. You're not asthmatic, are you?' he asked with some concern as she began to audibly choke. 'Sorry, I didn't recognise the signs of outrage,' he said sardonically as her dark gaze swept in loathing over his face. 'Admittedly I was being opportunistic just now,' he confessed, with a frank and open grin she didn't trust for one second. 'But I had wondered what it would be like to kiss you…actually I'd been wondering a lot.'

The suggestive drawl made her throat grow dry. 'And now you know.' Her chin inched up to a defiant angle. 'Sorry it was an anticlimax.'

Did he actually think she'd be flattered or aroused that he'd been thinking about her. Her mind swerved from the ambiguity of her present chaotic feelings, of which arousal was a very significant component.

'Now I know,' he agreed gravely. Noticeably he didn't deny the anticlimax part. 'You should wear gloves, you know. Your hands are like ice.'

Eve didn't need reminding how he knew the temperature of her fingers. When she'd linked her arms around his neck her fingers had been in contact with his bare flesh. She could recall quite clearly how warm his skin had been under her fingers—how the springy short hair there curled against his nape.

'So that…that…' She just couldn't bring herself to say 'kiss'. 'It was inspired by curiosity rather than a desire to show your ex what she's been missing?' she observed in a choked voice. 'What are you doing now?'

'Warming your hands,' he explained, placing her hands in the pockets of his jacket. 'Don't struggle, there's a good girl, someone might be watching.'

'Good, and if they've got a spare strait-jacket—even better!'

With her hands confined in the deep pockets of his jacket she found herself standing chest to chest with him. Still understandably jittery after being kissed, she found the experience almost claustrophobic. If she'd extended her fingers she could have touched the hard flesh of his thighs through the thin layers of fabric. The molten feeling in her belly spread insidious tentacles through her body.

She would definitely have curled her hands into tight balls to avoid this very situation had he not inserted his fingers into the palms of her hands. His thumbs were inscribing overlapping circles in her palms. The sensation it created was almost electrical. 'Almost' didn't enter into it, she admitted as the ripple of feeling reached her toes!

'There, isn't that better?' he was saying as she fought against the cotton wool consistency of her brain. 'What's wrong, Eve? Do men normally ask your permission before they kiss you?'

'Not formally, but I'm usually a willing participant,' she informed him thickly. 'Has it occurred to you yet that you've put me in a very awkward position?' It was just occurring to *her* that there were ramifications to this situation beyond the collapse of her nervous system. 'The Atkinsons probably won't want me to work for them any more.'

'Why? Have you killed off their prize Busy Lizzies?' He took her hands from his pockets, as if the idea had been his and she hadn't been ramming her nails in his palms. 'Circulation restored,' he said, gifting her back her hands, which showed an alarming tendency to tremble.

She wrapped her arms across her breasts in an instinctively protective gesture, one which he observed with a hatefully knowledgeable smile. 'They might not like the hired help kissing the prospective son-in-law. I happen to get a lot of work by word of mouth. My reputation is important.'

'That has a deliciously archaic sound to it. Does this mean you only kiss men after a formal arrangement has been reached?'

'I'm talking about my *professional* reputation.' It was easy for him to act as if this was all a joke, but she'd won her clients the hard way. 'I think my personal reputation can take the strain of one feeble kiss, even from someone like you.'

'*Someone like me?*' The arching eyebrows shot upwards. 'You notice, I hope, that I'm willing to let the slight on my masculinity pass. It's all part of being in touch with my feminine side,' he drawled drily.

His expression softened quite unexpectedly, and Eve found the sudden caressing warmth hazardous. 'Relax, Eve. I'll make sure there are no unpleasant repercussions,' he told her confidently. 'I'm grateful for the favour, truly.'

She believed him. Just like that. She had the strong gut feeling he just didn't waste his time saying things he didn't mean or throwing away boasts he couldn't back up. Sarcasm and sharp words she could cope with, but consideration had a deeply detrimental effect on her. For some reason she felt an aching emotional lump in her throat. This was silly. Why was she letting this man mess about with her emotions?

'You make it sound,' she burst out, 'as though I offered my services! I thought merchant bankers were all sickeningly rich, boring, grey little men,' Why, oh, why hadn't Uncle Drew been just that? 'But you're stark staring mad. The most deranged individual I've ever met!' she elaborated. 'I don't want your gratitude. I just want to get out of here and go home.' Dear God, I'm the one who sounds deranged, she thought, hearing the unattractive shrill note of panic in her voice.

Anyone would sound shrill, wouldn't they, if they'd discovered something they'd just been too stubborn or scared to admit to earlier? Drew Cummings wasn't just an attractive man, *she* found him disturbingly attractive, and not just in an objective sort of way!

There was definitely nothing objective about the taste of him in her mouth. She drew a shaky line over her trembling lips with her tongue. This had to stop now. Drew Cummings was a very unsuitable sort of man to be getting interested in. Even if there had been the remotest chance of anything coming of this he was also a man who was about to be reunited with his only true love, she reminded herself brutally.

The moisture had dried off her full pink lips almost immediately, but it had reminded him of the sweet moistness of her mouth. 'I'm relieved you don't think I'm boring, but...' he touched his temple '...I *have* spied the first sprinkling of grey.'

Eve found herself automatically searching his thick blond hair. She detected the faintest hint of auburn—he was almost strawberry blond in some lights—but no grey. Drew Cummings was one of those golden people, and there was another one inside the house waiting for him. Two of a kind.

'Are you going to move your car for me, Uncle Drew?'

'There you go again,' he growled. The woman was making him feel positively elderly.

'Sorry,' she said with a patently unrepentant smile. 'In our house you are always referred to as Uncle Drew.'

'It worries me no end that I'm referred to at all in your house.'

'The man,' she continued, 'who wrestles lions before lunch and brings about world peace in the afternoon.'

'Daniel...' he began, his brows drawing together in a fierce frown.

'Thinks the sun shines out of your...whatever,' she added hastily. Anatomical references, however lighthearted, had a tendency to make her mind wander in unhealthy directions. Actually, he did have a very, very nice rear end. 'He worships you,' she amended swiftly, privately appalled at her wantonly lustful thoughts. 'And here you are about to get into some heavy romantic reunion just when he needs your attention,' she observed disapprovingly.

'Is that how it works with responsibility? I've often wondered. You put your own life on hold and take a vow of

chastity for good measure. You must have a very understanding boyfriend, Eve. Have you never heard of balance?
All work and no play,' he goaded softly, 'makes Eve a very
bitter and frustrated young woman.'

'I'm not the least bit interested in your sex-life,' she retorted, and the less interest he displayed in hers the happier
she'd be. She didn't want to be reminded that she'd taken
a few liberties with Theo's name.

'Really?' he drawled with undisguised scepticism. 'I got
the distinct impression you were *very* interested in my sex-
life. We've shared such a lot in so short a time. I know
your boyfriend can't kiss, and you know who was my
first...' The suggestive quirk of his lips made her blush
madly and he laughed out loud. 'Such instantaneous rapport
is rare. I feel as if I should consult you before my next
move. Should I play hard to get or...?'

'I could care less!' she yelled back hotly. He really was
the most sarcastic pig she'd ever met. 'I should go in, if I
were you, or you'll just be plain late rather than fashionably
tardy. I'm sure you never do anything that is unfashion-
able.'

'That's me, a victim of fashion and the distressing need
to conform,' he agreed blandly, with all the confidence of
someone who never tried to gratify anyone's expectations
but his own. 'Talking of fashion.' His eyebrows lifted as
he looked her up and down. 'If you ever want a few tips...
Actually,' he said glancing at the heavy stainless steel
watch on his wrist, 'I *should* put in an appearance now. I'll
just move the car. And don't worry. I'll keep you up to
date with any developments in my love-life.'

Whistling softly to himself, Drew decided he had every
intention that Eve Gordon would be personally involved in
future developments.

CHAPTER FOUR

'WHAT are you two plotting?' Eve, fresh from a hot bath, strolled barefoot into the kitchen. 'Has anyone seen my slippers?' She'd treated herself to a long, luxurious soak and was feeling benevolently disposed towards the world in general—even her brother.

Neither of the two boys replied to her original question so she knew she'd accidentally struck gold—they were up to something. Do I really want to know? she wondered, with a cowardly unwillingness to disrupt this glow of well-being.

'That's a really nice dress, Evie. I don't think I've ever seen it before. It does something for her, don't you think, Dan?'

The dress in question was a jersey tunic top in bright red that reached to mid-thigh. Nick had to have seen this item from her limited wardrobe at least a hundred times before.

'What are you after?' She addressed the question to Daniel, knowing she was more likely to get the truth out of him than her brother. Thank goodness Daniel was recovering from his embarrassment—at least he hadn't dashed from the room, as he had on the last two occasions they'd met, but his gaze did slide awkwardly from her own.

'Spit it out, Nick,' she advised, wriggling her behind comfortably onto the table-top and swinging her chilled toes clear of the tiled floor.

'We've been discussing our eighteenth.'

'Oh, well, Daniel's welcome to come too on Saturday. It's not really a party,' she explained apologetically. Her budget didn't stretch to anything more than a nice meal for

family and friends—not that they had any real family ex-
cept Great-Aunt Emily, who had refused her invitation. No
big surprise there. As far as Aunt Emily was concerned
becoming a *man* wasn't something to celebrate! She
thought there were too many of the creatures around to
begin with. Eve, who was quite fond of the eccentric old
lady, had been quite relieved. Emily and Nick did nothing
but squabble when they were within shouting distance of
each other, and being a referee could get tiring.

'Dan's come up with this idea of combining our cele-
brations.'

'Well, it wasn't really me, it was Uncle Drew.' Daniel's
glance shifted to Eve's left. 'Perhaps he'd better explain.'

It was about halfway through this halting explanation
that Eve realised there had been three people in the kitchen
when she'd entered, not two. She was suddenly very conscious of her long bare legs and the fact she had nothing
other than her pants on under the clinging tunic. To her
horror, just knowing he was there was enough to send a
burning flood of tingling to her breasts. She didn't dare
glance down to see if the evidence of this physiological
anomaly was as explicit as she suspected.

Thinking about Drew Cummings, let alone being in the
same room as him, made her more aware of her body and
its needs than she'd ever been in her life. She'd been going
along a happily unaware sexual sleepwalker until she'd
been unwillingly awakened by the wrong man. In this case
ignorance had definitely been bliss!

Stiffly and reluctantly Eve swivelled her head. Sure
enough there he was, in the far corner, examining the
crowded, untidy noticeboard. What did he think he was
doing, lurking in corners?

'How long have you been here?' She resisted the feminine impulse to smooth her hair or do anything fluttery and

revealing. Had he been watching her? The idea made Eve feel disturbingly vulnerable.

'I gave the boys a lift over.' He was fingering a shopping list written in Theo's bold, but illegible print. The black jeans and dark cashmere sweater he wore emphasised the long, lean lines of his powerful body. It's shallow and silly to get worked up by a good body and a pretty face, she told herself severely, especially when it's attached to such a provoking personality.

She was going to deal with this bizarre attraction in a mature and adult manner. At least she would once she'd worked out what mature adults did about these sort of situations. For now she'd just make do with pretending it wasn't happening. He didn't seem to be in any hurry to look at her at all. Obviously I'm not nearly as fascinating as I think, she decided with a self-derisive shrug.

'Becoming a taxi service to teenagers can be a full-time job if you're not careful.'

'I'm always careful.'

And now wasn't the time to forget it, he reminded himself firmly. He didn't need to worry; he was in control; he knew exactly what he was doing. Besides, it was no skin off his nose to combine the parties.

He'd obviously been too cryptic for his own good. Eve was looking at him as though he was talking gibberish. She looked after her brother, who was a handful and a half, and as far as he could see her work amounted to manual labour in all weathers. It was ridiculous to expect a girl this young to shoulder so many responsibilities.

He felt a stab of anger for the parents that had left their children so inadequately provided for. Drew could deal with lust, he was no green adolescent, but what was going on with this protective stuff? Let's face it, Eve was possibly one of the least vulnerable females he'd ever met, but, despite the proud self-sufficiency, she had a soft centre. It

was hard now to realise he'd thought her a hard-boiled little
nut that first time. She was the last woman in the world
who would want to be cosseted and protected. *Protected!*
His thoughts skittered to an abrupt halt. What am I, un-
hinged?

What's he frowning at me for? He wasn't very careful
when he gave his heart to Charlotte Atkinson, was he?
Eve's lower lip pushed forward resentfully at that unpalatable thought, and she began to chew angrily at the soft
flesh. I suppose everything's rosy there again. She felt suddenly alarmed by the jealous shape of her thoughts.

'It does seem foolish to duplicate a birthday celebra-
tion—same guests and so forth. Don't you think? I've hired
the Crown for Saturday night.'

'I doubt if it would be a duplication. Nick's just having
a special family meal.' Did he think they needed charity?
She linked her ankles and swung her legs, pendulum-like.
Her toes brushed the cold tiles and she didn't notice.

'I've organised music and so on, and a few family and
friends to put a damper on an evening of unrestrained
youthful debauchery.' He exchanged a quick grin with the
two boys and continued as if she hadn't spoken.

It was the first time he'd seen her legs without a covering
of some sort. The skin was breathtakingly smooth and flaw-
less. The muscle definition in her rounded calves was as
taut as a dancer's. When she'd strolled into the room he'd
realised there was something very individual about the way
this girl moved—a natural grace that captured and held the
attention. Well, his attention anyway!

'But there's a problem with the catering.' He cleared his
throat. The skimpy red thing, whilst not clinging as such,
did reveal the supple slenderness of a very excellent body.
The fact that her sensuousness was innocent and not studied
only intensified the effect. 'Nick tells me you could cope
with that. It would get me out of a hole.'

The Crown had informed him they wouldn't contemplate under any circumstances an event with outside catering. Their stiff necks had done some rapid bending when he'd offered to pay the full price and provide the food himself.

Eve looked indignantly towards her brother.

'Well, you're a great cook with basic stuff,' he responded defensively. 'And Theo's brilliant. He loves nothing better than feeding people, and he's bound to help if we ask him nicely.'

We could be safely translated as *me*. 'I don't like being manipulated, Nick. And save the hurt spaniel look,' she advised. 'It doesn't work on me.'

'Not often,' Nick agreed cheerfully. 'But it was worth a try.'

'Theo's a chef?' The muddy rugby shirt Drew had lifted from the overflowing linen basket was several sizes too big for Nick. 'And a big bloke too.'

'Theo? Rugby?' Nick chuckled softly to himself at the idea.

'That's Sam's',' Eve said crossly. 'And I'd prefer it if you didn't go through my dirty laundry.'

'*Your* dirty laundry? I thought you said this was Sam's.' How many men did Eve Gordon have? he speculated irritably. He'd just decided to rescue her from a social vacuum—not entirely out of the goodness of his heart, admittedly—and she had men crawling out of the woodwork. Which from what he'd seen could do with a lick of paint— or several! Close to thinking the whole idea had been stupidly impulsive and was just too much damned hard work, he looked round the room with disfavour.

'Sam is our lodger,' Nick explained helpfully. 'We've got three, to make ends meet.'

Next he'll be discussing my overdraft arrangements with the man, Eve silently fumed. 'I'm sure Mr Cummings isn't interested in our domestic arrangements, Nick,' she reprimanded her brother sharply.

'It's no state secret, is it?' Nick muttered in a disgruntled tone. Eve was being more unreasonable than usual.

'Talking about domestic arrangements, Evie, you've used up all the hot water again, my love.'

'Theo!' She'd entirely forgotten he was home.

'Yes, Theo,' he repeated, shooting her a slightly quizzical look. 'And you must be…?' He looked towards the big blond chap who was watching him with a curiously antagonistic expression.

'Drew Cummings.'

'Uncle Drew! At last! We've heard a lot about you.' A Greek god in the flesh in her kitchen obviously went some way to explaining Eve's somewhat peculiar behaviour.

'All I've heard about you is you're *not* a chef or a rugby player.' He looked just the type to have Eve washing his shirts too, Drew concluded, swiftly summing up the boyfriend and being under-impressed with what he saw.

'I can confirm both those statements. Especially the rugby part. However, it's possible I might well have been a great chef in a previous incarnation,' he said, grinning at Eve, who still had that slightly hunted expression on her face.

'Theo works at the university,' Nick explained.

'In the Psychology department,' Eve added, getting to her feet and tucking herself in at Theo's elbow. She wondered if she should link arms with him, but on balance concluded it would be best if she acted as naturally as possible.

Any minute now someone was going to say something, and Drew would know what a fraud she was. He'd know she'd invented a boyfriend and, worse still, he'd know she'd *needed* to invent him. If he doesn't find out I'll never…*never* lie again, she promised fervently.

'He's a professor,' Nick added for good measure.

'Really?'

From his neutral tone it was hard to tell what Drew was thinking, but Eve knew that most people looking at Theo's grey-flecked beard and shoulder-length dark hair tied back in a leather thong didn't immediately associate him with serious scholarship. His clothes were usually shapeless, and today was no exception. But even with his somewhat individual bohemian approach to style Theo was an attractive man, in a distinctly Southern European sort of way.

He was also forty-one, divorced, and not lucky in love. One rainy night about four years ago Theo had confided, after he'd emptied a particularly good bottle of red, that the woman he loved was married to an invalid husband she wouldn't leave. Eve thought Theo deserved some good fortune on the love front.

'Nick thinks we can supply food for a joint birthday party at the Crown. I've already told him we've made alternative arrangements.'

'The Crown.' Theo nodded approvingly. 'Very posh. But I'm surprised they aren't doing the catering themselves.'

Eve could have stamped in vexation. When it came to interpreting body language Theo was remarkably slow.

'It was a last-minute booking and they have a staff shortage,' Drew explained glibly.

'You wouldn't expect anything too fancy…?' Theo's interest was obviously whetted.

'Theo, we can't… I mean…' What do I mean? she wondered, aware of the curious looks being directed at her. 'We couldn't possibly impose on your good nature.'

'Why? It's never stopped you before. I'm just joking, Evie,' Theo said, puzzled by the look of anxiety on her face. He threw an arm casually around her shoulder and drew her to his side. 'You wanted to give Nick a party and this seems the ideal opportunity. You know I'm up to the challenge, sweetheart.'

For 'affectionate grin' Drew read 'leer', and he felt vaguely queasy.

One swift glance towards Drew was enough to confirm Eve's suspicions. Anger flared. Where did he get off being all fastidious about a bit of harmless naughty word-play between two people he thought were lovers? In point of fact they weren't, and Theo's words had lacked any hidden meaning, but that was irrelevant.

'Besides, you could do with letting your hair down.' Theo affectionately ruffled her short locks. 'What there is of it. Now, I'm afraid I'll have to love you and leave you, folks. I've got a meeting I'm late for. Looks like we'll meet again, Drew. If you get your skates on I'll give you two a lift down to the sports club,' he said, switching his attention to the two boys.

'Badminton!' Nick banged his forehead with the heel of his hand. 'I was so busy helping people...'

'What a hero.'

Nick grinned, and ignored his sister's wry interjection. 'I almost forgot. Cheers, Theo, that'll be good. Come on, Dan. See you later, Evie.'

'In before ten-thirty,' she responded automatically as the room rapidly emptied—almost. The 'almost' was significant enough to send a secret shiver down her spine.

'Will he be?' He read the perplexed expression in her deep brown eyes. 'In by ten-thirty.'

'Oh, I expect so.'

How had she somehow ended up **alone** with him? Despite being an innocent bystander to **the circ**umstances she felt absurdly guilty, almost as if she'd **stag**e-managed the event herself. It wasn't as if she *wanted* this to happen, she told herself. The situation was making her feel physically ill.

'It felt strange at first, laying down the law to someone

only a few years younger than me, but Nick's quite considerate in his own way, and very mature for his age.' A frown creased her smooth brow. Sometimes she worried he'd had to grow up too quickly. 'If he ever strays off the straight and narrow I'll always know it was his idea. He's not a very malleable individual,' she added drily.

'You seem to have got the balance right.'

'Is that a compliment?' She widened her eyes in exaggerated shock.

He gave an almost sheepish shrug. 'It looks like it,' he confessed. 'As I'm being so nice, aren't you going to offer me a drink? It would be the neighbourly thing to do.'

'We're not neighbours.' She didn't think she trusted him when he was nice.

'I'm injured.'

'Not trivially, I hope.'

'That was petty.'

She grimaced in acknowledgement. 'I know, but you… you…'

'Bring out the beast in you?' he suggested mildly.

'You should be so lucky,' she sniffed.

'I know.'

Her eyes clashed with his: her own filled with shocked dismay, his with warm irony—very warm. The sort of 'warm' that could make a girl say and do stupid things.

'Mind if I join you?'

Eve had retreated to her perch on the table once the room had emptied. 'Can I stop you?'

'At any point.'

'I don't know what you mean.'

'You know *exactly* what I mean,' he contradicted smoothly as he slid beside her, his long legs stretched out in front of him. He appeared totally relaxed. 'The boyfriend has a trusting disposition.'

'It's one of his charms,' she agreed huskily. Her heart

had taken on a scarily irregular rhythm. 'One of many,' she added with a hint of desperation.

'But then again, why should he worry, leaving you alone with me?' he agreed blandly.

Eve knew his eyes were fixed on her profile, but she kept her own gaze fixed firmly on her hands, which lay neatly folded on her lap. 'Precisely.'

'How long have you and he been together?'

'Theo has lived here for nearly five years.' The other lodgers had come and gone, but Theo never had.

Drew inhaled sharply. 'Five years!' His lips tightening in disapproval. 'You must have been young.'

'Eighteen.'

'I suppose it's understandable if you had a father fixation,' he observed harshly. 'But I'd have thought you'd have worked through it by now.'

'Theo has always been my friend when I've needed him.' Stung to anger, she finally looked at him. All the disdain she had heard in his voice was on his face, and then some. 'I respect him.' I don't care what he thinks, she told herself firmly.

'There's a hell of a lot more to a relationship than respect and friendship!' he snorted dismissively.

'Perhaps if there had been a bit more friendship in your relationship with Lottie she wouldn't have ditched you so dramatically.'

'Oh, we had friendship aplenty.'

Eve didn't understand the odd, bitter inflection in his voice.

'I did say I'd keep you up to date with developments, didn't I?'

'I'll pass,' she responded gruffly. The last thing she needed was a blow-by-blow account of their tender reunion scenes! Or maybe that was *exactly* what she needed to bring her to her senses!

'To understand the present you need to have a working knowledge of the past. I'm not exactly sure how much of the nitty-gritty details you know.'

'What am I?' She raised her hands palm up. 'A captive audience? The way I hear it you've got enough money to afford professional counselling.'

'Perhaps I prefer your gentle sympathy. And then again…'

'You're the sort of person people dread sitting next to on a train or plane. The sort who feels obliged to supply their life history. I don't care if Lottie found out you were having affairs by the dozen or she couldn't stand your snoring.'

'Actually, I was just too boring and predictable for her,' he said in a matter-of-fact way. 'You see, she shares your view of bankers.'

'She thought *you* were boring?' *She* couldn't have heard him right. Drew Cummings was many things, but boring was not one of them.

The sombre expression died abruptly from Drew's face and a laugh of genuine amusement was wrenched from his throat. 'I'm really flattered by your incredulity, Eve. Close your mouth, darling,' he advised softly. 'It's a very tempting target.'

'Oh…!' Her mouth closed with an audible snap.

The thought of what her mouth tempted him to do brought a film of perspiration to her upper lip. Dry-throated, she swallowed convulsively. How would he kiss her? Hard, his mouth hot and hungry? Or would it be slow and subtle? Her eyes half closed as for a split second she was floating. She could almost feel his tongue…taste… A tide of intense heat swept over her body and she gasped. She'd become nothing short of shamefully depraved. Where would this tendency to depravity end? That was the worrying question.

He was watching her with keen-eyed interest, and she

had a nasty feeling telepathy might just be included amongst his talents.

'Did she actually say that, at the church?' she asked, clearing her dry throat noisily. What a prize bitch the woman was.

'Not in the church vestry—nothing so dramatic. She rang me the night before.' His sexy mouth twisted in a bitter smile. 'From the airport, five minutes before her flight left. I got the idea she wasn't leaving anything to chance.' He gave a sardonic smile.

She hadn't even had the guts to speak to him face to face! He was definitely due a bitter smile or two, she reflected, astonished that he could relay the information with so little display of emotion. On second thoughts she didn't trust his composure; nobody could recount that sort of history and not feel devastated.

'That really stinks!' she exclaimed frankly, her bosom swelling with indignation. 'Even if it was true—the boring bit.'

He was looking at her really oddly, and she remembered, belatedly, that she was probably bad-mouthing the woman he loved. 'I don't mean to offend you, and I'm sure she's a very nice girl...' she said stiffly. If you like that sort of thing. 'But it's a really horrible thing to do to anyone.'

'Even me?'

'I wouldn't wish something like that on my worst enemy.'

'I take it you wouldn't jilt your man?' Drew was watching her with a disturbing half-smile, languid but oddly alert.

'I wouldn't be stupid enough to get myself as far as the church with a man I didn't want to live with for the rest of my life.'

'Things aren't always that cut and dried.'

What am I? Too young and inexperienced to know that? Eve stared at him, her dark eyes smouldering. Was he actually defending what the woman had done? He must be besotted, she decided angrily. I'd never forgive someone who did that to me, let alone consider a reconciliation. Why am I so angry? The question stopped her dead in her tracks.

'We knew each other almost too well. I thought I knew what she wanted.' He massaged his jaw and looked into the distance, his gaze unfocused. Eve found she resented the fact his thoughts were obviously a long way from her.

'It came as something of a shock to discover that the thought of growing old with me was giving her nightmares. If we'd talked earlier, who knows?' His wide, powerful shoulders lifted slightly. 'As it was, Lottie just freaked at the thought of forever after with me.'

Lottie wasn't freaking out now, Eve thought, recalling the older woman's eager anticipation of his arrival. 'Not talking is not my idea of *too* close; it's not nearly close enough.'

'Well, if we're talking close, your Theo wasn't exactly intuitive back there. You all but spelt it out in semaphore that you didn't want him to help with the party. All you got was a pat on the head. He treats you like part of the furniture.'

'It's called being at ease with someone. Not everybody displays their feelings in public. What did you want him to do? Throw me on the table—' she patted the hard wooden surface '—and make mad, passionate love to me?'

The image her sarcastic words conjured up took the edge off Drew's sense of pleasurable anticipation. He'd come here with the firm intention of kissing Eve Gordon again. He had taken some trouble to ensure he had a legitimate reason to be here. The knowledge that his intellectual objectivity was taking a back seat to his obsessive lust was not a comforting thought.

'Not everybody has any emotions to display in private. How old is the guy anyhow?'

'He's exactly the right age,' she declared, tossing her head and smiling.

Drew's nostrils flared. 'Does he often criticise you like that? Don't you mind?' he asked incredulously.

'Criticise…?' She wrinkled her nose. 'I didn't notice.'

'That crack about your hair. There are a lot of men around who persistently denigrate the way their women look, and the women just take it. I didn't think you were the type.'

'He doesn't care about the way I look,' she responded unthinkingly. 'That is, Theo isn't interested in superficial things like looks,' she added hastily.

Eve didn't much like being classified as a subservient appendage. She could vaguely recall some teasing comment, but things Theo said to her weren't indelibly engraved on her memory. She didn't lie awake at night replaying their conversations word for word. Whereas every sentence and phrase that had passed between her and this man had been dissected and analysed in minute detail during the wee small hours.

'Some older men like to get a young woman. They're more malleable, easier to brainwash.'

'Theo's never taken advantage of anyone in his life!' she gasped indignantly.

'I think your hair suits you short. You've got a good neck.' The words took her totally by surprise.

It had sounded too abrupt and terse to be a compliment, but she could see his smouldering glance was still fixed on the graceful curve of her throat. She felt strange and breathless. Her neck had never made a man look hungry before.

'Thank you,' she rasped. Her skin prickled where his eyes touched.

It didn't look as if her gratitude or the contemplation of her neck was affording him much pleasure, so maybe the prickling meant her neck had come out in nervous blotches—it felt like that.

As she struggled to stop herself touching her throat, the indentation between his brows deepened further. 'Does he know about me?'

'He knows all about Uncle Drew. I've told you, we all do.' She adopted a light, teasing tone and rolled her shoulders to relieve the tension coiled there.

'I mean does he know about *us*?' It seemed Drew was not feeling humorously inclined.

'There is no us…'

'Yet.'

If his confidence was meant to unnerve her, it did. What had he said? He didn't let his libido rule him; he just enjoyed it. And does he intend to *enjoy* me? Is it really that simple for him? Probably. She was sure that Charlotte was the only woman he'd ever been emotionally attached to. Eve also knew she didn't have the emotional objectivity that was required to have an affair with Drew Cummings. She didn't even want that sort of objectivity. Neither did she want a man still tied to his past.

'For a man who wants to make up with his old girlfriend you have a kind of unique way of showing it.'

'I don't want to discuss Lottie,' he said dismissively.

You and me both. 'It's a bit late in the day to say that. I've had chapter and tragic verse!'

'I didn't realise you were jealous.'

'I'm… I'm…'

'You don't need to be,' he told her soothingly. 'My relationship with Lottie is—complicated. My relationship with you is much more straightforward.'

'I really admire your ability to compartmentalise your life, Drew,' she sneered. 'I don't know what you're suggesting, but—' she began.

'Yes, you do. I find you sexually attractive and you find me...'

'Arrogant beyond belief!' she gasped. Lottie was intended for deep, meaningful relationships and she was good for a quick...! Did he even know he was insulting her? 'What would I want with a man who's obviously trying to prove himself to be irresistible to all women just because the one he wanted did a runner?'

'That's one theory certainly,' he agreed in a composed manner.

'Are you still in love with her?' She felt like cringing the moment the words were out of her mouth. To her amazement he paused for a second and appeared to consider her question seriously.

'Some things are hard to put into words.' He hadn't had much difficulty up to this point! 'I don't quite understand why you're taking the moral high ground here. Why am I getting the grilling? I'm not the one living with someone. I'm prepared to accept that.'

'You're mad.' She wriggled to the edge of the table, but he leant across and grabbed her by the wrist. 'Do you mind?' she said, looking pointedly at his fingers curled around her slim forearm. 'The last time you did that...' she reminded him.

The last time she had been wearing suitably protective underwear and his sinewed forearm hadn't been pressed across her aching breasts. Or perhaps her breasts hadn't been aching then. Either way it seemed to be an inescapable fact that her hypersensitivity to this man increased alarmingly every time she saw him.

'I won't mark that lovely skin.'

'I prefer you didn't touch the "lovely skin".'

He grinned, leant close, and cupped her face almost casually in his free hand. 'Liar.' His thumb traced the faint hollow beneath one cheekbone. 'Tell me, why were you so anti the idea of joining forces for the boys' birthdays?'

'We're not a charity case. I may not be able to afford to hire the Crown, but we've got by up to now without any hand-outs from you!' Her voice was gruff and aggressive whilst inside she was melting. He probably knew about the melting; he was experienced in such things—the dramatic rise in body temperature, the intermittent tremors that afflicted her tense body.

She closed her eyes because his face was too close, and she could feel the inexplicable warmth of tears prickle against her eyelids. She couldn't shut out the masculine fragrance of him, though; it filled her flared nostrils. His thumb had stopped moving, but it still rested lightly against her skin.

'I told you, you'll be doing me a favour.'

'That's another thing. This whole thing smacks of *Upstairs, Downstairs*!' she accused wildly. She couldn't say the more she was in his company the more she liked it, could she? Though life would be simple if *liking* really did cover the way she felt about him.

He'd released her wrist now, and suddenly both hands framed her face. Eve could feel the merest whisper of his lips against her own. The delicate skin covering her eyelids quivered, but they remained tightly closed.

'Will I be expected to keep out of sight with the rest of the hired help?' Her voice sounded as though it was coming from a long way off. She gave a shuddering sigh, and the fingers that had intended to remove his hands clutched at the soft wool of his sleeves.

Drew looked at her fingers, tightly curled in the dark fabric, and his eyes gleamed with savage satisfaction. His breathing deepened and quickened as he rested his chin against her forehead. His lips moved softly in her hair. Through her eyelashes Eve could see the outline of the strong column of his neck. The intimacy was shattering, like nothing she'd ever known or dreamt of. She wanted to lean closer and press her lips against his throat. What would he do if she did? What would he do next anyway? She knew she was trembling and clinging, and doing all the things she'd decided to definitely avoid, but for the life of her she couldn't stop.

'I wanted to see you again.'

'And you can't understand why?'

'I didn't say that…'

'Well, your tone more or less implied it.'

'I admit I was surprised by how much I wanted to see you again. Our last meeting left me wanting more.' His throaty voice was as exciting and erotic as his embrace.

Or does he just want to use me to make his Lottie jealous? 'We shouldn't be doing this,' she whispered.

'Because of Theo…?'

He still thought she belonged to someone else, but it hadn't stopped him. He thought she was the sort of woman who would kiss him while committed to another man. He probably thought she'd do more than kiss! Perhaps his opinion of her had changed less since that first meeting than it seemed.

He didn't mind if she was that sort of woman because that was the sort of woman he'd wanted since Lottie had deserted him. He wanted the sort of woman who took love-making as light-heartedly as he did. She didn't…she couldn't. From things Daniel had dropped it was pretty clear that Drew had established his reputation as a lady-slayer. She didn't want to be one in a long line of willing victims.

She wasn't sure yet, but she might just be falling in love with Drew Cummings, and he was almost certainly still in love with his ex-fiancée. Sleeping with him would be a quick route to disaster.

Eve suspected the quickest way to make him stop would be to tell him the truth. Words like 'love' would have him running for the hills! Ignoring her initial impulse, she swallowed the truth. She allowed her lips to brush his throat just for a fraction of a second. She was conscious of the faint, salty dampness of his skin, and then she pulled back.

'I don't want to do this,' she lied. She wondered whether he'd actually be true to his word.

His body stiffened. There was a slight pause in which Eve, her mind racing, had several frantic thoughts about retracting her firm statement. It might make her look fickle and indecisive, even a tease, but, hell, wasn't that better than feeling like a martyr? She hadn't a single martyrish instinct in her entire body; suffering did nothing for her. What could be so bad about a fling with the sexiest man she had ever met—or would ever meet? she thought, busily rationalising.

'Now she tells me.' He ran both hands rapidly through his hair and then paused, wrists under the angle of his jaw, fingers linked behind his head

It was the last response she'd expected. To her total amazement he moved casually away from her. When he'd said he would stop she hadn't thought he'd keep his word with such insulting ease. She knew she was being perverse, but she couldn't help it.

He might at least have pretended to be in the grip of unreasoning passion! The impression that he could take it or leave it while she was coping with the most gut-churning sense of deprivation she had ever experienced left her dignity in tatters.

He stood up and ran a hand through his hair again. She suddenly realised that he wasn't as unstressed as he'd sounded. His suffering couldn't compare with her own, of course, despite the taut expression on his face and the nervous tic in one lean cheek. The drawn-out, tense look to his lean body was a dead giveaway. *Relief, Eve? I've obviously finally lost my marbles,* she concluded.

'It probably wouldn't be a good idea,' she said weakly.

'You don't have to apologise for using your right of veto.'

'I wasn't!' she flared indignantly.

'*Probably* isn't a very definite term. "Probably" is closely associated in my mind with "perhaps" and "possibly".'

'That's because you're thick-skinned.'

'An eternal optimist would be a kinder way to put it, but we won't argue about it.'

'I thought that was what we were doing.'

'You're a very pedantic person. Has anyone ever told you that? Are you afraid of kissing me in case you discover you enjoy it?'

'I've already been kissed by you, remember.' She already knew she'd enjoy it. That was the problem—or one of them.

'You call that a kiss?' His deep, derisive laugh rang out.

'Now who's being pedantic? And we all know why you kissed me then.'

'Actually,' he said thoughtfully, '*we're* not entirely sure on that one.'

'Sure!' she scoffed, stifling the uncertainty his unexpected statement had created. There was nothing more pathetic than a woman who heard what she wanted to, she told herself sternly. 'This is an entirely ridiculous conversation to be having.'

'I agree. We ought to be doing it, not talking about it.' A warm, dark hole had replaced what had once been her stomach. She swung her heels too far underneath the table, lost her balance and had to stagger ungracefully to her feet.

He watched her acrobatic demonstration silently. His fleeting enigmatic smile made Eve uneasy.

'Not that I have any problem with verbal lovemaking—it has its place and it can be very stimulating, don't you think?' He paused politely for her to offer an opinion, inclined his head slightly when she didn't respond and continued smoothly. 'I could tell you right now, for instance, what wanting to kiss you is doing to me—physically speaking—if you'd like?' His voice had been transformed into a deep, toe-curling purr.

'A generous offer,' she croaked, 'but if you don't mind I'll decline.' I might be coming down with flu. That would explain the febrile symptoms.

'I could say it's your loss, but it wouldn't be true. I rather think it's *our* loss. Does your sexuality embarrass you, Eve?' he enquired, looking at her flushed cheeks and shocked face. 'You know you're not in love with your shrink, don't you?'

'He's not a psychiatrist; he's a psychologist.'

'A teenage girl should not chain herself to one man before she's had a chance to live. Any man with an ounce of decency wouldn't want her to,' he added grimly.

'I'm not chained to anyone.'

'Prove it,' he responded immediately.

'Let me guess how…' Despite everything, she felt her lips twitch. 'You've got to be kidding, Drew!' His name came naturally and satisfactorily to her lips. 'What a line!'

'Crude, I agree,' he conceded, holding out his hands in culpability. 'God, girl, what do you expect? I'm pretty desperate here. You'd condemn me to a cold shower?'

His rueful honesty was incredibly seductive. It moved her more than any pretty speeches. She could feel her defences crumbling beneath the weight of his outrageous sincerity.

'Cleanliness is next to godliness,' she reminded him primly. Does he really want me this much, or is he just damned persistent?

'Well, you should know about cleanliness. It appears you do the laundry for half the town.' He nudged the laundry basket with his toe.

'Everyone in this house does their own laundry,' she corrected him. 'I'm not some sort of domestic drudge, you know.'

'Possibly not,' he conceded, with very little conviction, 'but you must admit you haven't led the normal carefree existence of the average teenager. This can't have been what you'd planned for yourself. You must have felt envious when you saw your friends spread their wings, leave home, go to university?'

She wasn't even conscious of nodding. At first she hadn't been able to read Alice's letters without feeling a sense of envy. They'd planned to share a flat together. It should have been *her* complaining in letters about the noisy flat above, the essay she'd had to work on until four a.m. Each incident had been something that might have happened to her had things been different. Only things hadn't been different, and Eve wasn't the sort of person to lament for long.

'I enjoy what I do,' she told him in a cold voice. 'And I'm no longer a teenager. I haven't been for some time. Neither do I need you to show me what I've been missing.'

'Nick will be leaving home soon,' he reminded her, immune, it seemed, to the venom in her voice. 'He won't need you,' he said brutally.

Eve wondered if he was being deliberately cruel. She lifted her eyes to his and instinctively shied away from the flicker of compassionate understanding in his eyes. She didn't want his pity; she was no charity case!

'I know it hurts to be redundant, but you've done too good a job of making Nick independent. Are you going to use your freedom—take the opportunity to do all the things you weren't able to before? This place, for instance.' His glance encompassed the high-ceilinged room. 'It's a white elephant, and you know it. The upkeep alone must be enormous. If you sold up...'

'I realise that your financial advice must come pretty dear, but I'll pass. And *you* actually have the cheek to accuse Theo of trying to influence and control me? Though not to his face, I notice...'

'Naturally not. I'm terrified of the man...' Drew drawled wryly.

'I wasn't thinking of physically,' she snapped, her eyes spitting fire. 'It's a sorry state of affairs when a person is measured by the size of his muscles!'

'I see. It's the man's intellectual prowess you admire so much. You think I just don't have the smarts to exchange insults with the professor. What do ya know? My mental mediocrity has caught me out again,' he sighed.

'You're...you're...so *smug*!' she exclaimed in exasperation.

When they'd handed him out a perfect body and a face most females, given the option, would attach to their dream lover, he'd also received a mind like a steel trap and a tongue that was too articulate for his own good! And didn't he just know how to use the package!

'You know I'm right. That's why you're mad.'

His air of composed common sense and restraint made her want to scream. She took a step closer to him and jabbed her shaking finger in his face. She'd have given a great deal to shatter his cursed insouciance.

'What right have you got to lecture me?' she demanded hoarsely. 'Why are you so bothered about what I do anyway?'

An expression she couldn't quite decipher flickered momentarily into his eyes, which remained fixed on the finger that danced before his nose.

'Damned if I know.'

He suddenly reached for her outstretched hand and firmly

pulled her extended finger towards his mouth. As his warm lips closed moistly around her finger Eve let out a sharp gasp of disbelief.

Just when he'd lulled her into a false sense of security with all that up-front, painful honesty he did something sly and manipulative and mind-blowingly *sensational* like this!

At the first touch of his mouth a debilitating weakness invaded her limbs and incapacitated her brain.

'Drew…' Most of the protest didn't emerge in her voice. In fact what came out was alarmingly near to an appeal, a request.

'What?' he whispered throatily as he proceeded to give each separate digit individual loving attention. He hooked her by now limp arm around his neck and, reaching for her waist, jerked her closer.

She found herself leaning against the hard contours of his body. And he was hard—hard, powerful, lean, and very different from herself. Who'd have guessed, she mused dreamily, that a contrast could be so fascinatingly pleasurable? She was suffused by warm, voluptuous sensations. It felt so perfect, so *right*.

Her body seemed to know all the right moves before her sleepy, amorous brain had even got into gear. Unconsciously her hips rotated, slowly, suggestively grinding against him until their lower bodies were sealed. Drew murmured something indistinct and she felt the aggressive masculine thrust against her belly. Excitement spilled out, licking along her nerve-endings like fire. Drew grunted, his fingers splaying in the small of her back, moving to softly explore the taut curve of her bottom and making her gasp.

Kissing distance, she thought, languidly lifting her face automatically…eagerly to his. All her antagonism had been submerged by the tangible white-hot sexual charge that had exploded between them.

Drew dropped his head until their lips were just a whisper apart. His eyes were half closed. She gazed, transfixed by the tiny dancing flecks of silver in his molten blue glance. He was breathing hard, his breath warm and fragrant against her face. The warmth of his body smelt... male, alien, exciting. Eve's body was strung out with the hungry anticipation of his touch. She lifted the hand at her side and it came into contact with the outer aspect of his thigh.

'S...sorry,' she gasped with revealing naïveté as she felt the extraordinary contraction of heavy muscles beneath her fingertips. This display of quivering muscular tension had evaporated the last drop of moisture from her throat; she couldn't swallow now, let alone speak.

'No apology necessary.' Perhaps his throat was dry too. She hardly recognised the thick tone. 'I like it.' The tip of his nose brushed the side of hers. 'That's it,' he approved as her fingers with slow-blooming confidence returned. She felt his chest vibrate with a deep groan, and a small smile of female triumph curved her lips.

But she couldn't smile while his teeth were tugging gently at her lower lip. All she could do was utter a series of indistinct guttural moans before his plundering lips silenced her completely.

The taste of him exploded in her mouth as his tongue probed deeply. She could taste his urgency and arousal. Her hands hooked around his head and her fingers burrowed deep into the lush thickness of his hair as she responded with an answering hunger and the desire to strain frantically against his lips.

Hands on her buttocks, he lifted her fractionally, drawing her up on tiptoes as he pulled her roughly against his arousal. The deep, driving need blanked out all intelligible thought from her mind. She pushed her hands under his sweater and let them glide against the muscle-packed flatness of his belly.

'You feel…'

'You like?' he asked, equally huskily.

The grin only lasted a split second before he had swooped to taste her again, with all the fervour of a starving man. But if she'd been in her right mind Eve would have been very disturbed by the brief flash of ruthless triumph: Eve wasn't in her right mind at that moment.

The frenzied hunger which made her touch, cling, provoke and sultrily demand by turns was outside the realm of her experience. She was barely conscious of sitting on the table-edge, his hands still beneath her behind. Her body arched backwards as his mouth bore her downwards.

She wasn't quite horizontal when the noise jerked her out of the sexual thrall. In retrospect, she realised it must have been a very loud noise, because nothing else would have penetrated her pleasure-saturated mind.

'Eve, I'm…we're…' Sam glanced to his fellow lodger with an agonised expression of appeal. He was standing amidst the broken shards of a jug that had been sitting on the old Welsh dresser. 'We wouldn't have… We didn't know…'

'We're very sorry, Eve.' Honor Wilson's face was bright pink, and her eyes darted around the room in studied avoidance of anything incriminating. 'Come on, Sam.' She tugged urgently at his arm, but Sam appeared to be frozen to the spot by the spectacle before him. 'We were just going to my room. *Weren't we?*'

'What…? Oh, yes, indeed. You won't know we're here. Nice to meet you…er… Yes, well, goodnight.'

'I take it I've now been introduced to all the inhabitants of 6 Acacia Avenue?'

Eve focused on some point over Drew's shoulder. She hardly noticed her well-toned stomach muscles begin to protest at the fixed, unnatural posture her body was frozen into.

The tableau was broken as Drew withdrew his hands from beneath her and straightened up. Eve, who was abruptly conscious of her ridiculous position, half reclining on the table, jack-knifed into an upright position and pulled frantically at the hem of her tunic, which was hitched up well above decency level. On the scale of cringe-makingly awful situations this had to be off the scale!

'That was Sam…' What would they think. I know exactly what they'll think, she thought bitterly. That I was rolling around semi-clad with a stranger on the kitchen table. They'll think that because that's what I *was* doing! I'll emigrate, she decided, swallowing a bubble of hysteria, to Siberia.

'The broken nose was a giveaway—rugby player.'

'And Honor.' It was a bit late for self-recrimination now. Damage limitation was the name of the game.

'They're a couple?'

He didn't miss much, did he? 'No announcement has been made, but I think so.' The postgraduate engineering student and the librarian were not one of life's most obvious teamings, but it seemed to work for them.

'Perhaps you should start a dating agency. I take it there's not much point me trying to carry on where…?' Eve made a choking sound 'No—right. The mood's been broken.'

He sounded remarkably philosophical about it. She'd heard men of her acquaintance sound more emotional about the cricket score! Her body was aching with frustration and he was as cool as the proverbial cucumber. The man was a bloody robot, she fumed, nursing a deep sense of resentment. She wasn't going to give him the satisfaction of seeing how mortified she was, how he'd turned her world upside down. She was going to tough it out.

'This won't happen again.'

'I should hope not,' he agreed readily. 'I know some folk

are big on outlandish locations, and spontaneity has its place, but I'm a soft bed and locked door man myself—boring, I know, but there's much less chance of interruptions.' He glanced thoughtfully at the table-top. 'Your poor back would have been covered in bruises.'

The image his words conjured up rubbished her cool composure act in seconds. Her face went scarlet. She opened her mouth to speak and nothing came out but a gurgle.

'I wouldn't actually have...' The words emerged croakily past her semi-paralysed vocal cords.

'If you say so,' he agreed indulgently. 'I think this officially makes me *the other man*, don't you?'

'Will you please go away?' she pleaded.

When he did she wasn't as delighted as she should have been. If she hadn't been so financially straitened she might just have indulged in a childish orgy of crockery-smashing.

CHAPTER FIVE

EVE walked into the foyer and almost collided with Daniel. 'Hello, Dan. Happy birthday.' She nodded in a friendly way to the pretty dark-haired girl who had her arm linked in his.

'I'm glad to see you…Mi…erm…Evie.' For a minute there Eve had been sure he was going to say Miss. She hid her smile and felt suddenly geriatric. 'Thanks for the birthday present, It was…cool. I thought you weren't coming. Nick said you were, but I thought maybe…'

The dark-haired girl tactfully detached herself at that moment and gave Eve a shy half-smile before turning up the voltage in Daniel's direction. 'See you inside, Dan?'

'Definitely.'

'She looks smitten, Dan.'

He blushed some more, looked pleased, and shrugged a lot. Eve kept her expression suitably grave. 'I thought maybe you were still mad with Uncle Drew or me.'

'I was never mad with you, Dan.' He looked so relieved he obviously hadn't noticed she'd not extended her amnesty to his uncle.

'Uncle Drew was great about it once Nick explained. He even came up with the idea—and it worked.' He saw her blank expression and smiled. 'You know—about you being his girlfriend and me trying it on and him—Uncle Drew, that is—being mad as hell. It worked like a charm,' he concluded happily.

Nick hadn't told her about this development, but then nobody had ever accused her brother of being dumb. 'Clever old Uncle Drew.'

'I know. He's great, isn't he.' Daniel responded enthusiastically. A frown creased his smooth brow. 'That's why I'm so worried. I'd hate it if he got, well…hurt. He *seems* all right, but I don't know what Mum will say when she gets back,' he said with an anguished look.

'Why's that?' Eve enquired dutifully. She knew from experience when a sympathetic ear was required, and he had the look of a boy who needed badly to get something off his chest.

'This woman is back—the one who…' He broke off suddenly and looked confused.

'The one who dumped your uncle?' Eve suggested calmly. Some of the bubbly excitement that had been zinging around her bloodstream started to slowly dissolve.

Daniel gave a sigh of relief. 'You know all about her. I'm not supposed to talk about it, but if you know… Mum calls her "That little…"' His face grew red. 'Well, that doesn't matter.'

'I don't think you can be held responsible for your uncle's personal life, Daniel.'

'I know that, but…after she dumped him, Uncle Drew went a bit crazy, you know. He packed in his job, gave all his suits to a charity shop and went backpacking around South America.'

No more champagne blood. No more happy bubbles. 'A somewhat extreme reaction,' she agreed quietly. She couldn't imagine the strong, confident, irreverent Drew she knew being so devastated. The woman must have meant everything to him. She could only imagine the emotional turmoil he must be feeling now—seeing her again.

'He even grew his hair long.'

'Not his hair?' she gasped, hiding her extreme distress with a display of flippancy. 'Did they call in a psychiatrist?'

'It was serious,' Daniel responded reproachfully.

Eve didn't need telling. She recognised 'serious' when

she heard it. She recognised 'broken heart' and 'shattered life' too. 'Sorry. Do you think he's...they're...?' Her expression carefully concealed any personal interest she might have in the reply.

'I don't know,' Daniel admitted unhappily. 'He had lunch with her, and she keeps ringing him—at all hours. He might even have seen her more often. I don't know. What if...?'

'Stop it, Dan,' she said firmly. 'Your uncle is a big boy now, and nobody's going to hold you responsible if he does decide to get back together with his old girlfriend.'

'I know, but...'

'You're worried about him, I know, and it makes you a very nice person. Try not to be. Will you do that for me?'

'I guess so,' he agreed.

'I don't think you should keep a pretty girl like that waiting too long, do you?'

He blushed scarlet. 'She is pretty, isn't she? Thanks, Eve.'

Eve watched him leave with a visibly lighter heart and she envied him.

'I can certainly understand your concerns now I've met him, Drew.'

Eve recognised the mid-Atlantic accent immediately. The night *could* get worse! She hovered uncertainly, her hand still on the curtain that half concealed the entrance to the cloakroom. If composure was as easy to apply as lipstick she'd have been out of there ages ago.

So much for avoiding the woman at all costs. Lottie had known Drew and his family for ever; of course she was going to be here. The party was a perfect place to make their new understanding public property. If they hadn't reached an understanding yet it wouldn't be for want of trying, if Daniel's facts were accurate. Had the trying reached the bedroom yet? Eve's stomach churned with nauseous rejection at the idea. Her indecision had only lasted seconds, but she felt as though she'd been furtively hiding there half the night.

'Nick?' The sound of Drew's deep voice made her freeze. Her knuckles turned white against the rich velvet drape as she strained to hear the rest of the conversation.

'He's quite a character.' Eve instantly loathed the other woman's laugh; it had a false, empty ring to it. 'It's going to be hard to discourage the friendship. If you want my advice, I…'

'It's not the friendship I…'

Eve swept the curtain aside with a dramatic flourish. There was a loud swish and a rattle of brass curtain rings which granted her their immediate attention. She stepped out, her body rigid with fury.

They were discussing her brother, who apparently was considered unsuitable friend material for his precious nephew! How *dared* they? Nick was worth ten of any teenager she'd ever met. There was a short expectant silence before Eve managed to get her anger partly under control. Her bosom was still heaving dramatically against the silky cowl-neck bodice of her brand-new dress, but the furious tears had reversed down the tear ducts and she had control of the strong impulse to bang their interfering beautiful golden heads together!

'If you don't think Nick is good enough to be Daniel's friend what the hell is tonight about? Is it our social standing that doesn't match up to your standards? The female of the sub-species is all right for the occasional grope, but you wouldn't want your son to marry one? You hypocrite!' she erupted furiously.

Drew's eyes swept in a distracted fashion over the full length of her slim body as the furious words spilt out.

'Hypocrisy,' he corrected her, 'is when you pretend you don't like being groped.'

If she'd been red-faced earlier Eve was now paper-white with fury. If he thought she was going to be sidetracked by a bit of ogling or slimy innuendo he could think again. And if he leered at her again she'd tell him so!

'There's no need to get shrill. Daniel's just worried about Nick's influence...' Charlotte began in a soft, placatory voice.

Shrill indeed! She ain't seen nothing yet! Eve fixed her with a glare guaranteed to wither, and the older woman's lips acquired a pinched look of anger.

'Nick, a bad influence!' she jeered. 'That's ridiculous! How *dare* you make a judgement like that? What gives you the right?' She addressed the question to Drew as her voice rose a quavering octave in the space of a single syllable. 'They've been friends ever since Daniel moved here. His parents obviously have no objections. What makes you such an expert on adolescents all of a sudden?'

'Good question, Drew. One amongst many this conversation raises.'

The tall blonde was still wearing a calf-length trenchcoat underneath which Eve could see the glitter of silver lamé. She was looking around the trio with interest.

'I take it you're Nick's sister; I can see the family resemblance. I can't imagine why we haven't met before. I wouldn't take any of Drew's criticism to heart, my dear.' Katie Beck cast her brother a maliciously sweet smile. 'He's always been very opinionated.'

As far as she could see Drew wasn't evincing any of the nervousness of his elder sibling he'd once claimed. If anything he appeared to view the interruption with resigned irritation.

'I'm sure Lottie will back me up on that point. Lottie...such a surprise,' she drawled languidly. It was impossible to tell from Daniel's mother's voice if the surprise was pleasant or not, but in view of Daniel's comments Eve suspected not. 'This seems to be the night for surprises.'

'You managed to get back in time, then,' Drew said with a noticeable lack of enthusiasm.

'I wouldn't have missed it for the world. I changed in the taxi.'

'I take it you're not alone.' Drew looked around with a frown.

'Alan's around somewhere,' she confirmed vaguely. 'I've offended his notions of decency by stripping to my undies in the taxi; he can be a shocking prude sometimes.'

'A prude and an exhibitionist. Quite a combination.'

'He's gone in search of an immediate stiff drink,' his sister responded with a lazily good-tempered grin.

'He's not far away then—good. And I'm sure you can't wait to see your son. Incidentally, Dad and Faith are here somewhere. You won't mind if I leave you for a few minutes? I need to sort a few things out—in private. Eve!' he barked peremptorily. He looked at her expectantly, waiting for her to fall into step at his side.

'When he snaps his fingers I come running.' Nostrils flared, she gave a tinkling derisive laugh. *Unbelievable!* Eve rolled her eyes at this display of masculine conceit. 'You've got to be joking…ouch!' she yelped indignantly as he fixed a heavy arm firmly around her waist.

'Well…well,' his sister mused, her eyes dancing with amused speculation as she watched the angry young woman being dragged unceremoniously away by her brother. 'What do you make of that?' She looked at the silent woman beside her.

There was no reply forthcoming, but from Lottie's expression Katie got the impression that whatever the answer was, it was making her feel pretty pig sick. There is some

justice in the world! she thought, hiding her jubilation behind a bland smile.

'Tell me, how's your husband?' she asked sweetly.

It was keep up with him or fall on her face, because he
wasn't shortening his stride. Reluctantly Eve did the for-
mer.

'Where do you think you're taking me?' Anxiety at the
prospect of falling over her floor-length gown made her
voice sharp. 'Will you...?'

'In here looks all right,' Drew interrupted, after pushing
a door open. He flicked on a light switch and bustled her
inside. His tight-lipped expression was that of a man who'd
used up all his tolerance. 'This'll do,' he confirmed, closing
the door behind them.

'This is private,' Eve protested, looking around the small
office. Add a small room and Drew Cummings and you
had the ideal formula for instant heart-thudding claustro-
phobia.

'Exactly.'

The stark fluorescent light was the sort that emphasised
every shadow and line on a person's face. Her meticulously
applied make-up might just compensate for it, but she
doubted it. Not that it mattered any more. Drew was here
with his Lottie and he was a two-faced snob! Daniel's rev-
elations made their new beginning sound very cosy.

Naturally the light revealed no nasty surprises on Drew's
face; he still looked as beautiful as ever. Her heart gave a
little skip, but she ignored it. She glowered disdainfully at
him and lifted her chin.

'I *am* worried about Nick's influence on Dan.' He didn't
waste any time with preliminaries. 'Hold on and let me
finish,' he added hurriedly as she started to puff up once
more with indignation. 'Only not the sort of influence you
think. Nick is a remarkably charismatic character.'

Takes one to know one, she thought miserably. She'd made a poor job of pretending, even to herself, that she hadn't been waiting with breathless anticipation to see Drew tonight. Helping Theo lay out the buffet earlier, she'd been as jumpy as a nervous teenager.

Exasperated Theo, who hadn't been his usual imperturbable self today, had eventually sent her off home early to get changed. It all seemed so foolish now—the breathless anticipation, the taxi because she'd taken so long getting ready she'd missed her lift! Drew's sister had got dressed in the back of a car and she looked sensational! As for the extravagant new outfit—which, she decided, probably looked to Drew's more experienced eye cheap and nasty beside Lottie's designer label—what a waste of time!

'Dan rides around on the coat-tails of his popularity. He's completely in his shadow—a situation he finds very comfortable. Dan's a great kid too, in his own way. Only his way isn't as flamboyant or up-front as Nick's. I just think that Dan tends to be, for want of a better word, plain lazy. He'll let Nick have all the ideas, Nick do all the organising; he'll sit back and be organised.

'I just think he should be a bit more independent. There isn't always going to be a Nick around to smooth his path in life. It would do his self-esteem no end of good to do something occasionally for himself. None of that,' he said firmly, 'reflects badly on Nick. He looks after his mates; that's admirable. The last thing I'd try and do is try and put an end to their friendship. Some of the most enduring friendships I've made go back to my schooldays,' he added thoughtfully.

It didn't take a genius to interpret this as an obvious reference to Lottie. Eve felt suddenly painfully excluded. That sort of shared history was something she couldn't compete with, even if she had felt the inclination to do so.

'All of which I would have explained if you hadn't

zoomed in like an Exocet missile.' Drew thrust his hands in the pockets of his formal dark jacket and leant back against the wall, his unwavering blue eyes fixed on her face.

'But *she* said…' Eve persisted. She felt somewhat deflated by this comprehensive and thought-provoking explanation. She had to admit there was some justification to Drew's concerns.

'Lottie.'

'Whatever.' She dismissed the name with a sniff. 'She said…'

'Nothing that is out of context with what I've just explained to you.'

'You've discussed this with her?' Don't be stupid, Eve, of course he has. The pair of them were obviously getting back to where they'd once been. It might take time, but he'd virtually told her straight out they were soul-mates. It was as well she knew for sure now, before she'd done anything foolish, she told herself briskly.

'I mentioned it in passing,' he agreed. 'God knows what you'll be like in defence of your own offspring.' The lines around his eyes deepened with sudden amusement, and Eve struggled to dismiss the vision of blonde-haired infants with deep blue eyes.

'I'm not counting on finding out in the near future.'

'Or at all?' he asked, his voice unexpectedly harsh. 'I was doing the classical male thing and assuming you'd want a family eventually.'

'Well, actually, I do. But as I'm hurtling towards twenty-five, not thirty-five, I don't feel any great sense of urgency. Is there anything wrong with that?' she enquired, a hint of pugnacity creeping into her voice.

'You may be a baby, but your boyfriend's on the wrong side of forty.'

'I've no intention of having Theo's babies!' she gasped.

The notion was the funniest thing that had happened yet tonight—probably because it was the *only* funny thing that had happened. So far the evening had been a non-stop disaster.

'Does he know that?'

'He probably suspects it.'

'Do you realise you were like a tigress when you thought we were putting the boot in with Nick? And he's only your brother. You've got some very strongly developed maternal instincts.'

'Me! What about you? I could accuse you of being over-protective with Dan, but *my* manners are far too nice.' She shot him a sweetly belligerent smile. 'And it's not as if Dan's even your responsibility—well, only temporarily. And you don't think *only* when there are just the two of you. It's not as if we've got surplus relations coming out of the woodwork.'

'I'll admit the strain of responsibility has probably gone to my head. Perhaps I was never emotionally equipped for parenthood.' The smooth skin of Eve's forehead creased. She didn't know what to make of the odd inflection in his voice. 'And now you'll no doubt say I'm too old.'

She threw him an impatient look. 'If you were female I'd say you were fishing for compliments.'

He shook his head reprovingly. 'What a sexist thing to say, Eve.'

'Actually, I don't think about it at all,' she lied fluently.

'Which? My age or fertility?'

'Neither,' she responded, in a dignified manner which only partly concealed her agitation. 'But you're not,' she added abruptly. 'Unless you're really an octogenarian with a really good cosmetic surgeon.'

'That was really very good,' he observed admiringly. 'You didn't come right out and say, How old are you? For you it was impressively subtle. Actually, I'm thirty-six.'

'Has *she* got children?' Wow! What happened to my *subtlety* then? Do I have to blurt out everything that comes into my head? she wondered, stifling a groan and blushing deeply.

'Are we talking Lottie again?' He sighed, in a bored sort of manner, but she could sense his wary withdrawal.

Oh, yes, she thought, it would suit him very well to avoid that subject. 'I expect you planned a family together.' She gasped, and clamped her hand over her mouth. 'I shouldn't have said that,' she said quickly, watching with some trepidation for some sign of his response. His expression was neutral, almost bland. 'You see, I have no social graces whatever,' she told him with a hint of belligerence.

'Yes, we did.'

Well, I asked for that, didn't I? she thought bleakly. It was easy for her fertile imagination to conjure a painfully clear picture of Drew losing not just the woman he loved but the life they'd planned together all in one fell swoop. She could see him dwelling over the years on what might have been—never finding anything to fill the place of what he'd lost. Now he had a chance to reclaim what had been his, rebuild his dreams. What man could resist that opportunity?

In her admittedly limited experience she'd found that trying to recapture and recreate youthful memories wasn't always what it was cracked up to be. But she could imagine what his response would be if she decided to share this piece of worldly wisdom with him!

'That was part of the problem.' Eve wasn't sure now if he was even aware she was there; the unfocused expression in his eyes gave the impression he was looking at something a long way off. 'I wanted a family and I assumed Lottie felt the same. She didn't say otherwise—not until…' His distant gaze focused suddenly on her face and he looked almost surprised to see her. 'You did want to know,' he taunted her, sweeping his hand through his hair. The weary gesture brought a lump of emotion to Eve's throat.

'I didn't mean to pry,' she whispered miserably.

'Then it looks like you've got more than you bargained for, doesn't it? You opened this can of worms, remember. I dated Lottie when we were both at school. We went to university at opposite ends of the country and we drifted apart; there were other people for us both. We met up again in our late twenties and eventually we moved in together. We had good jobs, a great social life. We were so compatible that most people envied us.' His words were laden with embittered sarcasm. 'You know how the story ended.'

If the story had ended. Eve didn't think it had.

'I was probably rude to her,' she conceded suddenly. Most people, herself excluded, had a history, but wasn't it just her luck that the man she had fallen for had come face to face with his history? It didn't help that the face was exquisitely perfect.

'*Probably?*' One eyebrow shot skywards.

'I've apologised.'

'*You have?* What for, exactly? I must have missed it,' he confessed apologetically.

'For spoiling your intimate moment,' she hissed. Perhaps he won't notice I sound like a jealous witch, she hoped— without much conviction.

'Intimate! You have a very peculiar idea of intimacy, Eve. In my intimate moments I don't discuss the hurdles of adolescence. We've shared what I would call an intimate moment, and you'll recall…'

'I wish you wouldn't talk about that!' she said urgently, clasping her hands together and beginning to pace back and forth in the confined space.

'Why not? You did, and you weren't talking—you were yelling at the top of your very efficient lungs, as I recall.'

He just had to remind me of that, didn't he? 'That was different,' she told him firmly. 'I was… I was…'

'Mad as hell?'

'Exactly. So it doesn't count. Actually I'd have thought you'd be grateful. She should be good and jealous now. Wasn't that what you wanted?'

'You tell me.'

'I'm sorry if I embarrassed you, but now, if you don't mind, I'd like to get back to the party.' A party she'd seen precious little of yet.

'I thought you weren't coming, you know,' he said, uncannily echoing his nephew. He stretched out suddenly and placed his hand heavily against the door she was about to open.

Like you'd noticed, she thought angrily. His voice was disturbingly close to her ear so she didn't turn her head. 'I had things to do.'

'Well, you did them very successfully. Nick said you hadn't finished getting ready,' he explained, when she shot him a quick questioning look over her shoulder. 'You look beautiful, Eve.'

'I wanted to make an effort for Nick's sake.'

'Not for my sake?' His sardonic gaze swept over her face. 'I'm disappointed. That colour really suits you. What would you call it—gold? It ripples when you walk…'

Her stomach did some unscheduled rippling too. Her sharp inhalation was audible as she spun around, her back pressed against the closed door, to face him. 'I'm not interested in getting involved with you, Drew.' If there had been such a thing as the power of thought her tense body would have passed through the solid wood.

'I think you are.'

'Then think again,' she advised grimly. 'You really expect me to amuse you until you decide to go back to Lottie? It's *obvious* that's what you're going to do!'

'Is that a fact?' he asked with interest.

Even he hadn't had the gall to deny it, she noticed. 'Of course it'll have to be when *you* decide. I expect a man has to salvage a bit of pride in a situation like this.'

'You seem to have thought this through very thoroughly. I notice there's one element you haven't included in your equation—your boyfriend. I use the term ''boy'' in the loosest possible sense here. He isn't an obstacle worth mentioning, it would seem—*interesting*.'

She'd been going to tell him about her little white lie tonight—*that* was how crazy she'd become!

'Perhaps I ought to tell your professor how *friendly* you've been with me.'

Now that would be one very interesting conversation. 'You wouldn't,' she said hopefully. She was going to have to confess to Theo about taking a bit of artistic licence with his name, preferably when he was in a good mood—a *very* good mood.

'How do you feel about blackmail?'

'A device employed by the scum of the earth,' she replied without hesitation. Drew's body was warm, with the quality of tensile steel and the texture of... She blinked rapidly. Most importantly, his body was almost as close as the sensual cloud that was attacking her judgement.

'Dance with me tonight and I might not mention your lapse in fidelity.'

'It's nice to have your first impressions confirmed. You *are* a scumbag!'

He gave a sudden incredulous laugh. 'You thought I was going to demand more than a dance, didn't you?' His eyes ruthlessly searched her face. 'Were you thinking of higher stakes than a kiss too?' He watched the telltale colour crawl up her neck until her whole face was aflame. 'Well...well, what a lurid mind you have.'

She made a sound of disgust and turned her head sharply

to shut out the amused glow in his eyes. 'Let me out, Drew.'

'Only out of the room, sweetheart, not my life!' He threw the words after her as she scurried down the hallway towards the sounds of people and normality.

'Have you met Dan's parents yet?' Theo placed his drink down on a table and caught hold of her hand.

'His mother.' For obvious reasons Eve didn't go into details. 'I've met Alan before.'

Theo ignored her reluctance and pulled her onto the dance floor. 'Don't be a killjoy, Evie, come on,' he urged.

'Are you drunk, Theo?'

He looked thoughtful. 'Not entirely sober is more accurate. I've reached a crisis point in my life.' Not you too, she thought, shifting her weight to compensate for his erratic manoeuvre to the left. 'And the alcohol was meant to clear my vision.'

'Is it working?' she asked, smiling with affection up at him.

'Not really. Sally rang me this morning.' He tried to sound casual and failed miserably.

The laughter died away from Eve's face. That explained his unusual tension today. She'd been so immersed in her own dramas she hadn't looked very hard to find the source of her friend's problem. Theo never spoke of the woman who had refused to leave her husband for him. She hadn't thought they ever communicated. He'd implied in the past that they'd severed their links totally.

'She's back in town. She suggested we meet.'

'Is that a good idea?' Eve asked reluctantly, her expression deeply sympathetic. He'd been traumatised so much by the relationship she didn't want to see him open old wounds, but she was very conscious that it wasn't her decision to make.

'She's living alone.'

'Has she left her husband?' Eve's eyes widened in surprise. 'He's not dead, is…?'

'No, he's not dead.' Theo said with uncharacteristic venom. 'The miserable beggar has left her. Yeah, unbelievable, isn't it? For his physio, would you believe! Irony doesn't get much darker than that, does it?' He gave a bitter laugh. 'Sally decides to do the decent thing and feels guilty as hell all this time—' his voice cracked with emotion and Eve lifted a comforting hand to his cheek '—and in the end he dumps her!'

'How is she?'

'It was hard to tell on the phone. It happened six months ago. Can you believe it? She didn't phone me until this morning. Do you think that's significant? What should I do, Evie?' he asked with an anguished groan.

Eve's eyes widened in dismay. He's asking me? She'd never felt less qualified to offer advice on emotional matters in her life!

'I mean, it's been a long time. People's feelings change. She sounded so…so impersonal. I'm not sure if I could hack being *just good friends*,' he confessed thickly.

'Have *your* feelings changed, Theo?'

She watched hope flare in his eyes and hoped to God she was doing—saying—the right thing.

'No,' he said simply.

'Then go for it,' she advised.

'I've nothing to lose, have I?' he said with a sudden laugh.

Only your sanity, she thought silently.

He placed both his hands on her shoulders and planted a loud kiss on her lips. 'Thanks, angel. Nobody will mind if I leave early, will they? Don't worry, I'll take a taxi,' he added with a grin.

Eve watched him disappear with a worried frown.

Across the room someone else had been watching this display of affection without any sign of the indulgent good-will displayed by people closer to.

'Drew, darling, do you remember when…?'

Half on his feet, Drew looked at the small hand on his sleeve and slowly relaxed back into his chair. He forced his facial muscles to relax too before he turned to his companion with a smile.

'Where's Theo off to?' Nick materialised at Eve's side before she'd found a spare seat. 'He looked like the devil was on his tail. He's been in a funny mood all day, have you noticed?'

Eve smiled affectionately up at her tall, gangly brother. 'I have, but I'm surprised you did. You're a sensitive old thing, aren't you?' she teased, ruffling his hair.

'Please, Evie, not in front of people. Keep the loving gestures to a minimum. I've got a reputation to preserve. I know you had doubts about tonight, but it's been good, don't you think? The combination of wrinklies and us seems to work.'

'I won't embarrass you by asking which category I come into.'

Nick grinned. 'It's made Dan's day that his folks are back,' he observed, flopping into a chair and dragging another one closer for Eve. 'They've invited me to stay the night. Are you cool with that?'

'Extremely cool.'

'The way I hear it you weren't so cool earlier,' he said casually. 'And Dan's mum seemed pretty interested in you. Is there any connection?'

'Daniel's mother is probably worried insanity runs in the family—especially as you're spending the night under their roof. When she arrived I was shrieking at Drew. It doesn't really matter why,' she added firmly.

Nick shrugged. 'If you say so.'

'Suffice it to say I made a fool of myself.' At the very least!

'It happens to us all.'

'What's this? Role-reversal? I'm the one meant to wheel out the homespun wisdom.'

'Not any more. I'm officially a grown-up and you, little sister, are a free agent. Just 'cos I don't often mention it doesn't mean I don't appreciate what you did—giving up university and stuff for me,' he said gruffly.

'If you don't stop,' she warned him, blinking back sudden tears and sniffing loudly, 'I'll be forced into another unseemly public display of affection and your street credibility will be zero.'

'In that case let's definitely change the subject. Who's the looker with Drew?'

'His ex-fiancée.'

'Ex? That's all right, then.'

'All right for who?' she enquired suspiciously as he got to his feet.

'You, of course. If you fancy the guy don't let an ex put you off.'

'I do not *fancy* anyone, least of all Drew Cummings!' She winced. As sophisticated responses went that one was probably on a level with your average year-niner.

If Nick knew, probably other people did too. She glanced over her shoulder, half expecting to see people talking about her behind their hands. Paranoia, Eve, that's all you need! If I ever needed my sense of humour it's now!

'I worry about you, sis,' Nick confided with a critical frown. 'Girls these days go for what they want. You shouldn't be so passive.'

I am not passive—am I? She shook her head, rubbishing this ridiculous idea. Admittedly she did apply a bit of a double standard in the dating area, and she just couldn't see herself asking a man out, but men had been using double standards themselves for so long she felt she was owed a few concessions.

Dating, as such, was not on the agenda as far as Drew was concerned. No, if she was to take the initiative she'd have to walk straight up to Drew and say— What would she say? Your place or mine? I'll supply the protection? I think not!

Drew hadn't claimed his dance, but then he'd had plenty of distractions. Did that woman always wear black? she wondered, glancing quickly over to the corner where Charlotte and her parents were seated. The cobwebby creation she was wearing covered a lot and cleverly revealed even more. Drew was still dancing attendance, as he had been all night. The older, distinguished-looking man had to be his father; the similarity was marked. They looked like a cosy family group.

Suddenly she couldn't take any more of it. She felt as if her head was going to explode. She plucked fretfully at her dress. The room was so hot she couldn't breathe properly.

Their combined laugher suddenly drifted across the room and something inside snapped. She couldn't keep up the pretence of having a great time for another second. If anyone asked her why she was leaving she was going to rely on the good old headache story—which was coincidentally true. By now she didn't much care if nobody believed her.

CHAPTER SIX

THE dark had never held any fears for Eve. Every shadow didn't contain demons in her imagination. She found the velvety blackness oddly comforting. It wasn't even that dark tonight. Even without the street lamps she would have been able to see—the sky was ablaze with the cold white light of a brilliant swathe of stars and the more mellow glow of a full moon. The silver luminescence was reflected against the frosty glitter on the pavements.

Her journey home skirted the park. She felt perfectly safe here; it was where at dusk or in the early morning she often jogged. Of course then there were usually other people around, jogging or walking their dogs. She didn't pause to consider whether her sense of security was realistic; she was just happy to have escaped.

It was good, she told herself, that she'd seen Drew and Lottie together. They'd looked good, as she'd known they would. Her original thoughts about Drew Cummings had been bang on target: he was definitely a shallow, egocentric rat. She couldn't imagine what had made her think otherwise! He hadn't spared a thought for her feelings when he'd continued his seduction campaign tonight. Was she to be the last fling before he trotted dutifully back to his childhood sweetheart?

The cry was eerily loud in the still night and for a split second Eve was distracted from her sombre reflections. After an initial moment of paralysed fear she identified the sound and her body relaxed.

It was only the plaintive cry of a cat. 'Idiot!' she said out loud, feeling foolish. The noise continued, and without really thinking she left the path to follow it. A few yards away she came upon the culprit, swaying amidst the top branches of an oak tree. The animal looked no more than a kitten.

'Here puss…puss,' she coaxed. 'You can't stay up there all night, it's freezing.' It soon became pretty obvious the animal wasn't budging. It was also pretty obvious if she stopped in one position for much longer she'd lose all feeling in her extremities.

Eve sighed, and wrinkled her nose in concentration. If she walked off and left the creature she'd spend the entire night worrying about its fate. Calling the fire brigade in the middle of the night for something that couldn't exactly be termed life-threatening seemed frivolous. There was only one option open to her.

She took off her coat and folded it carefully on the ground; it had been her mother's, and though not the latest fashion it was good quality. Her skin, previously protected by the heavyweight combination of cashmere and wool, immediately broke out in goosebumps. She shivered and wrapped her arms about herself as the cold bit deep.

'I hope you appreciate this,' she muttered as the cat let out a mournful cry. Teeth chattering, she lifted the skirt of her dress and tied it in a bulky knot above her knees. 'Right, here goes,' she said, selecting the easiest route up the tree in her mind's eye. Finally she stepped out of her shoes; heels were not meant for climbing trees. Mud adhered stickily to the fine denier of her stockings.

Long legs, natural balance and a good head for heights meant that Eve soon reached the stranded animal, despite the poor conditions and less than ideal equipment. There was no protection from the stiff breeze up amongst the bare branches. Eve thought longingly of warm open fires and regretted that the one in the sitting room of her empty house would be cold embers by now.

'Come on, puss.' At eye level now with the cat, Eve saw it was just a kitten, a tabby kitten. 'I'm not going to hurt you.'

Unfortunately the same couldn't be said of the cat. Her hand closed tentatively around the soft fur and the cowed bundle of misery instantly became a hissing fury. Eve let out a cry and recoiled as claws flashed before her eyes. She lifted her arm automatically to shield her eyes and felt her purchase against the branch loosen. Desperately she tried to stop herself falling. She felt herself crashing through branches before her fingers closed around a thin branch. Pain shot through the muscles in her shoulders as momentum added weight to her body and she swung pendulum-like from the insubstantial limb. It was only a temporary reprieve and she knew it. She felt her fingers slipping and heard the branch creak alarmingly.

'Let go, Eve, I'll catch you!'

If her situation had allowed for it Eve might well have given a sigh of relief. 'But I'm heavy.' And, she suspected, a long way off the ground.

'The branch is going to break. Just do it now!' came back the terse command.

'Now?'

'Yes, now!'

Eve took a deep breath, closed her eyes tightly and did exactly what he said.

'I told you I was heavy.' Panting, she rolled off Drew's supine form, her movements hampered by her long skirt, which had slithered back down to her feet.

He was sprawled lifelessly on the grass. 'Drew?' she got onto her knees and leant forward anxiously. His eyes were closed. She was almost relieved when an alarming rattling noise came from the region of his throat. Almost—it was a terrible sound.

'Drew,' she cried urgently, taking hold of his jacket lapel

and shaking him. She hoped it was the shaft of moonlight that had leached all the colour from his face. 'Are you all right? Stop that right now. You're scaring me!'

To her intense relief his eyes opened. He gestured towards his abdomen. 'Winded,' he gasped.

'Oh, is that all!' she gasped in relief. She slumped back on her heels and raised a trembling hand to her brow, which, despite the cold, was covered in a fine film of sweat. For an awful minute there she'd thought...

'All,' he croaked in a more recognisable voice. 'All!' He pulled himself into a sitting position. 'I'll be lucky if I've only got cracked ribs. That sort of thing looks much easier in the movies,' he reflected dourly. 'The hero clasps the girl to his manly bosom and strides off into the sunset with her expressing suitable gratitude,' he added pointedly. 'God, it was like being hit by a flying pig.'

'Thanks *very* much.' An analogy guaranteed to delight any female. 'I am grateful.'

'You sound it. Ouch...'

Eve raised her bunched fists to her mouth and ground her teeth into her knuckles as she watched him stiffly get to his feet. She snatched her hands away self-consciously when he looked at her and affected an appearance of studied nonchalance.

'Let me help you,' she said sharply, unable to maintain the pose as he grunted in pain.

'I'm fine, don't fuss,' he said, fending her off with one hand and brushing leaf mould off his dark suit with the other.

'Fine. Be strong, silent and stupid if you want to,' she observed tartly.

He looked at her, a smile dawning in his eyes. 'Do you know you're blue?' he asked, as she continued to shake convulsively.

'I left my coat over...'

Drew saw the coat before she did, and, taking a couple of steps towards the neat bundle, he picked it up. 'Come here,' he said, shaking out the garment, 'before you get pneumonia.'

Eve stood with her back to him and he slid the heavy coat over her shoulders. She gave a sigh of relief as she shrugged her arms in. 'I can't stop shaking,' she admitted.

Drew leant forward. Her head was tucked in the angle of his jaw. She could feel the firm pressure of his arms against her as he fastened the buttons.

'Thanks,' she mumbled. Once her nose got past the sharp smell of grass and leaf mould what she could smell was all Drew. The tantalising scent made her want to turn around and burrow closer, until it was all she could smell and all she could think about was him.

She abruptly walked forward out of his grasp. Beneath the big coat all that was visible was her dark head, slim ankles, and feet—bare feet! Drew looked at her slender back and then down at his own widely spaced hands which hadn't moved since she'd walked out of them. With a wry twist of his lips he self-consciously lowered them.

'What the hell possessed you?' he ground savagely.

'There was a cat—a tabby, I think.' She wobbled on one leg before regaining her balance as she pushed her foot back into one shoe.

'I'm not actually all that interested in the finer points of cat breeding,' he drawled nastily.

'It was stuck. I tried to rescue it,' she explained, looking upwards. She suddenly felt a little nauseous. Why hadn't she noticed earlier just how far up it was? If Drew hadn't come along when he had... She looked even more sick when it came to her in a blinding flash that she'd not been more surprised to hear his voice because at that precise moment she'd been praying for exactly that.

What's happening to me? I'm not the sort of lame-brain

female who waits to be rescued—I rescue myself. Admittedly her resources had been strained to the limit on this occasion...

'I don't see any cat,' he replied, looking around with elaborate interest.

'Well, I didn't make it up.' Did he think she did this sort of thing for pleasure? 'It ran away.' Not without leaving a memento; the scratches along her forearm were stinging like blazes now.

'It's not the only one.' His dry, almost impersonal observation made her glare at him suspiciously.

'Tactical withdrawal' had a much nicer ring to it. If he's guessed why I left so precipitately what will I do? Lie, she decided. What else is there for me to do?

'Cats always fall on their feet,' he continued, in a voice that no longer sounded quite so objective. Actually, she decided, sneaking a quick peek at his face, he looked halfway to losing his temper. 'Which is more than I can say for humans,' he added cuttingly. 'Logically, if the animal climbed the damned thing it could climb down.'

'Don't lecture, Drew. The poor thing was crying. I couldn't leave it, could I?' You'd have thought anyone with an ounce of decency could see the logic of her arguments, but from his expression it was obvious that Drew couldn't. The shadows highlighted the sharp planes and interesting hollows of his face, bringing to life an ascetic aspect she hadn't noticed until now.

'You climbed a tree in the pitch-dark, in sub-zero temperatures, barefooted...?' The words 'imbecilic' and 'deranged' hovered, unspoken but loud in the eloquent pause.

'Well, I could hardly climb it in these, could I?' she pointed out reasonably, stretching one muddy but elegantly shod toe towards him.

She studied him covertly from under the sweep of her thick but straight lashes. Whilst she hadn't been consciously trying to provoke him, she did feel a perverse satisfaction that he looked as though he was choking on his frustrated rage.

'Sorry about your suit.'

'The suit!' he snarled, looking at her as if she was insane. 'To hell with the suit! You could have killed yourself, and me too.' The muscles in his throat worked hard as he swallowed.

'I didn't ask you to catch me,' she mumbled, displaying what she knew was perilously close to childish truculence. Wishing didn't count as a request, did it? A confused expression suddenly crossed her face. 'How come you were here anyhow?' she asked with a puzzled frown. Confusion turned to anger as she met his guileless blue gaze. 'You were following me!' she accused hoarsely. 'Weren't you? What a creepy thing to do,' she said, shaking her head disgustedly.

'Lucky for you that I have creepy inclinations, isn't it?'

'You *were* following me then?'

'I saw you leave the party—alone and on foot. Tell me, Eve, does it strike you as a rational thing for a young woman to do in this day and age? Do you make a habit of exposing yourself to unnecessary risks? The doorman said you'd refused a taxi. He was quite concerned.'

'This from the man who abs…jumps off mountains and…and…' Her anger was intensified by the knowledge there was some justification to his observation.

'There's no comparison and you know it!' he snapped tersely.

'This isn't exactly New York. I was perfectly safe…' Her voice trailed away as she finally acknowledged she'd been nothing of the sort. In her right mind she'd never have done anything so impulsive—only it was becoming pretty obvious she wasn't in her right mind, and the reason for that insanity was at that moment looking at her as if she was crazy.

'How boring,' he drawled. 'I think going somewhere dull like New York would be a safer outlet for your adventurous instincts,' he drawled sarcastically.

'Have you?' she said abruptly, unaware of the sudden gleam of eager curiosity in her eyes. 'Been to New York?'

'I worked there for a while. Have you?'

Eve gave a sigh and hugged the heavy coat around her. 'No,' she admitted regretfully. 'I always wanted to travel, but I haven't got around to it yet.' Alice had wanted her to go backpacking around Australia after her finals, but she hadn't been able to leave Nick or the business.

There wasn't an ounce of self-pity in her voice, but something about its wistful quality made Drew very conscious of the freedom he'd taken pretty much for granted during his life—freedom to do pretty much what he pleased.

'But you will…?'

Despite Drew's harsh, almost angry frown, Eve thought she detected a hint of sympathy in his voice, and her chin went up in automatic defiance. 'Do you doubt it?'

'I don't doubt you could do anything you put your mind to.' The unexpected admiration in his voice made her forget how cold she was, but he had to spoil it. 'Perhaps I should take you to Central Park the next time you decide to risk your neck by playing Tarzan?'

Eve had a sudden insanely attractive vision of herself travelling to all the places she'd ever dreamed of. Her guide was the same person in all the exotic locations she'd frequently drooled over in travel brochures. The personal guide of her imagination had arresting blue eyes to die for, and all the drooling he did was over herself. She dismissed this piece of juvenile fantasising with an angry frown.

'If and when I decide to travel it won't be as an accessory. I'm afraid the strain of being an amusing companion would spoil the experience for me.'

'In my experience, Eve, sharing has a way of enhancing an experience.'

She couldn't take her eyes from the muscle that throbbed spasmodically in his lean cheek; it was like a time bomb, but much more aesthetically pleasing.

'Or ruining it,' she persisted stubbornly.

'I wonder to what extremes you're prepared to take this. Your honeymoon, for instance… Are you prepared to relax your prohibition then, at least?'

'Have I ever suggested I have any intention of getting married, now or in the future?'

His expression hardened. 'I see you can be realistic when you want to be,' he reflected drily. 'I saw the boyfriend run out on you. What's his idea of a romantic weekend break? He goes away and you stay home to iron his shirts?'

'Theo?' The after-effects of her little adventure were beginning to make themselves felt, so she didn't immediately latch onto his meaning. 'What? Oh, yes, he did have to leave early,' she said, sounding and feeling a bit vague.

Her knees had started to shake. There couldn't be a worse time for delayed shock to kick in! She needed all her wits about her now. If she gave in to natural instinct she'd be blubbing in his arms—his strong arms, with just the most perfect degree of muscle formation possible—and one thing might lead to another. She snapped her spine to attention and firmly banished the dreamy, moonstruck expression from her face.

'He doesn't seem the reliable type exactly.' His lips compressed into a thin sneering line. 'But then most women seem to put that fairly low down on their list of priorities in lovers.' His nostrils flared as he stared at her in disgust. 'I just don't understand you.'

'I didn't ask for your understanding.' The way things stood it was the last thing she wanted!

'You didn't ask me to catch you, but I did.'

'You dropped me,' she reminded him.

'I cushioned your fall,' he corrected. 'And it's likely I'll be black and blue tomorrow for my trouble,' he mused thoughtfully, pressing his hand to his flat abdomen. 'Come on, let's get you home,' he said as she stood there dithering with cold.

'I'm quite capable of getting home on my own.'

'Humour me, or I'll have nightmares about all the detours you might make on the way there.' He ignored her petulant expression and took hold of her elbow. 'Maybe you're happy walking through this Gothic landscape—' he looked thoughtfully at the skeletal black framework of branches above their heads '—but I'm made of softer stuff. I need someone to hold my hand.'

Eve's indignant gaze slid away from his mockery. He wasn't soft. Anything but. Recalling the steely promise of his body as he'd kissed her made her heart thud so loud she was worried he'd hear. But for the interruption she might well have had more to recall. Her shivers were no longer entirely due to the cold.

It occurred to her as they walked in silence the short distance to her home that anyone watching them would have assumed they were lovers having a late-night walk, doing the things that lovers did—kissing in the moonlight...

'Is something wrong? You kind of whimpered,' he explained as she raised her panicky eyes to his face.

'I trod on something sharp,' she improvised hastily.

'I won't waste my time telling you to be careful.'

'We're here,' she said in relief. She scrabbled through the contents of her evening purse to find her door keys.

'Do you mind if I come in?'

'Yes, I do!' Her eyes widened in horror.

'To use the phone. I left the party a little abruptly. I wouldn't want anyone to worry.'

'Oh, well…' The ironic gleam of amusement in his eyes made her feel even more wretched. He probably knew she didn't trust herself to be alone with him. 'Haven't you got your mobile with you?'

'Never on a social occasion. It's my token resistance to being eaten alive by the financial system. I let work take over my life once upon a time, but nowadays I strive for a little more balance.'

'Don't you like your work?' she asked, her curiosity whetted by his words.

'If I didn't I wouldn't do it,' he said with uncompromising certainty.

'But?' she prompted.

'But I don't need to eat and sleep my job, no matter how stimulating it is. Working excessively long hours, contrary to popular belief, isn't the sign of diligence, in my view it just means you're bad at time-management. You have to decide what's important—prioritise. I made the mistake once of equating a punishing work schedule with efficiency.'

Eve knew, watching the sombre shift of expression on his face, that he was thinking of his abortive marriage plans. What did Lottie make of the new improved version? she wondered grimly.

'Well, you'd better come in,' she conceded ungraciously. 'You can use the phone in here,' she said abruptly, as they stepped into the hallway. She gestured towards the console table.

Drew glanced up to the galleried landing. 'I wouldn't want to disturb anyone,' he said softly.

'That's all right. Honor's gone to watch Sam play rugby in Ireland—there's true love for you.' It occurred to her belatedly that she'd told him, unprompted, that she was alone in the house. He didn't even ask you, dumbo! When will you learn to keep your mouth shut? she silently despaired.

'Nick is sleeping over with Dan and your professor has gone walkabout.' Eve found the sardonic smile that curved his lips deeply disturbing. 'All alone, Eve?' he speculated.

'Uhuh,' she confirmed, as though she hadn't a care in the world. Don't over-act, girl, it's a dead giveaway. 'That doesn't happen very often.' She wasn't going to be spineless and surrender to outright panic. Pride forced her to put up at least a token resistance. 'I intend to enjoy the solitude,' she assured him defiantly, in case he'd missed the point.

'Then the professor isn't expected home tonight?'

'He didn't say,' Eve responded truthfully. 'Let yourself out when you're done.' *Please* she added as she vanished into the kitchen.

Eve flicked the heating thermostat on the wall, slipped off her coat and pressed the backs of her legs against the lukewarm radiator. It would be warm in a minute, and Drew would be gone. She watched the door, her body and mind torn apart by a tormenting ambivalence.

The sane portion of her mind wanted him to meekly go. She told herself he was probably anxious to make amends with Lottie for his hasty departure. On the other hand she'd never seen him display behaviour that could be categorised as *meek*. Her mind started feverishly working on what she'd say if he did walk into the room.

'Did you have a problem with the front door?' It was the first thing that popped into her head when he did appear, several minutes later.

'No, not with the door.' He didn't smile. His facial muscles didn't shift, even fractionally, to give her any clue to his mood.

The husky rasp of his voice ate deeply into her indecision. There was something mesmerising about his steady gaze.

'Is it anything I can help with?' All it lacked was a sultry pout, she thought drowning in a wave of mortification. A come-on—a blatant come-on, Eve. He'd certainly interpreted it as such if the smouldering approval in his eyes was anything to go by.

I can't believe I did that! What possessed me? As if I don't know, she mocked herself grimly. I bought that dress and went out tonight with the definite if undeclared intention of being seduced. Perhaps even doing some seducing, she accused herself angrily. It seems I don't even have the backbone to let my principles get in the way.

'Definitely,' he responded, without so much as the flicker of an eyelash. Her anger couldn't stand the impact of that voice—deep, suggestive, and mind-blowingly sexy. How could one word imply so much? Eve's body responded mindlessly and her brain wasn't far behind.

Under the circumstances she could understand the faint air of smugness about him. In a state of dry-mouthed anticipation she watched him walk across the room. He placed his hands on the wall either side of her face, his physical proximity finishing the job of snuffing out the last threads of resistance—as well as much of the light, with his shoulders.

She wanted him at any cost. Even if that cost was her pride. The frantic feelings of hunger were spiralling swiftly out of control inside her.

'Aren't they expecting you?' she whispered huskily. She couldn't bring herself to say Isn't *she*. His fingers were moving playfully through her hair and she felt dizzy, warm and excited.

'No.' He bent his head to nuzzle the area around her ear and her hands moved in mute, fluttering appeal before coming to rest, clenched tightly, at her sides. 'You look very beautiful tonight. You knew I was watching you, didn't you, Eve?'

'No.'

The husky, monosyllabic response was all she was capable of. His fingers were now toying with one shoestring strap on her dress; he was sliding it over the smooth curve of her shoulder and back again. His touch was whisper-like and soft against her skin. She gasped. The pressure inside her was building until she felt she'd die if he didn't kiss her—if she didn't feel his lips, taste…

She lifted her head abruptly, and, hooking her hand behind his head, yanked it down to her level. After the initial widening of shock Drew's eyes filled with sensuous delight. She felt the rumble of warm laughter vibrate in his chest. Her expression engrossed, she tilted her head first to one side and then the other, rubbing her nose along the side of his before fixing her lips against his. It felt so good to touch him…to smell him.

She relaxed against him as the pressure was gently returned and closed her eyes, deeply absorbing the unfamiliar texture of his lips. Even though the kiss was modest, Eve felt wildly daring. Taking the initiative was something she had never before contemplated doing. Surrendering to a man was something she'd never contemplated either.

'Open your mouth,' he said against her lips, and without thinking she did just that. She felt rather than heard the harsh groan that was ripped from his throat at her ready compliance. He cupped her face between his big hands, looked hungrily into her face and kissed her with bruising ferocity.

The raw force of his passion was more in every way than she'd imagined. She hadn't come to terms with her fevered response to this erotic invasion before she was suddenly conscious of cool air against her skin.

Hands flat against his chest, she pulled back just as the gold shimmering fabric collapsed with a rustle around her ankles. Her wide, startled eyes shot immediately to his face.

Drew's eyes were fixed on her body. travelling slowly over the entire slim length. He didn't seem to be breathing. When Eve looked downwards, it was as if she was seeing her own body for the first time through his eyes. She knew her body was firm and toned; she'd always taken her figure very much for granted. Now she was aware of every rounded curve and taut line. She felt the rosy peaks of her breasts pucker and tingle under his regard.

The lacy triangle of her pants and the silky hold-ups she wore seemed somehow much more intentionally provocative and erotic than complete nudity. Did he think she'd chosen them with this in mind? Had she, at some subconscious level? Her body was racked by shudders of a febrile intensity. Her senses were at fever-pitch as she waited for his gaze to reach her face.

When it finally did there was a savage exhilaration in his eyes that made her panic. A frisson of fear rippled through her. Is he seeing me, really seeing *me*? she wondered fearfully. He looked so…*driven*, and the desire in his passion-glazed eyes seemed almost impersonal.

'I didn't mean to scare you.' He ripped the loosened tie from around his throat and let it drop.

His words reminded her of his perception—scary at times, welcome now. She watched him tug impatiently at his collar, as though he was having trouble breathing.

'It's just you're so incredibly perfect. I'm not sure how long I can look at you without touching and stay sane.'

She felt her fears retreat abruptly. The awe in his expression was anything but impersonal. His desire made him vulnerable in a puzzling way. 'You can touch…'

The sight of his hand around the firm swell of one breast was intensely arousing. The warm, liquid movement deep in her belly became molten and actually painful in its intensity.

'Is this what chemistry feels like?' she asked, biting her lips to hold back the feral whimper that ached to escape in her throat. She gasped, and her body arched. The friction of his thumb against her nipple was slow and languorous.

'Only for the lucky few, I suspect.' His fingers slid into her sleek hair, providing the support her neck appeared unable to supply.

'I think perhaps I'm just a bit scared by the way I'm feeling,' she confessed huskily. Her fingers slid inside his shirt, and she caught her tongue between her teeth in concentration as she slipped several buttons with her thumbs. The hair on his chest wasn't dense; it had a soft, crisp texture. The satisfying firmness of the flesh underneath filled her with a delight bordering on delirium.

'How are you feeling?' he asked throatily as he insinuated one muscular thigh firmly between her legs.

She caught her breath sharply. 'I think I'm feeling you.'

His grin was fierce. 'You only think?' he growled, planting a series of open-mouthed kisses down the side of her neck before dragging at her swollen lower lip sharply with his teeth. 'I think we can do better than that.' He suddenly swung her up into his arms. He glanced at the kitchen table and shook his head. 'I'm hoping that you don't need the stimulus of exotic locations.'

'I've no serious objections to bedrooms.' This display of masculine domination shouldn't, in this politically correct, enlightened world, make her melt, but it did. Perhaps my hormones are less well educated than the rest of me? she theorised whimsically. She flexed her toes towards the ceiling and felt deliciously decadent.

'Give me directions.' He wanted to share the private joke that had brought the half-smile to her delicious lips—strangely he wanted to share everything, not just her body.

Her lips were made for kissing, he thought, his eyes caressing their full, sexy outline. Just thinking about those lips applied to even innocuous areas of his body made Drew want to break into a run and emulate an Olympic sprinter up the stairs.

He was as eager as a schoolboy. In fact everything he did with Eve felt new and fresh, and completely unblemished by the jaundiced boredom that had insidiously crept up on him recently.

Give directions! It struck her forcibly that if he was expecting any more than 'second door on the left' he was in for a big let-down. He obviously hadn't banked on fumbling tonight. Her laughter had an unsteady note to it.

In the act of kicking the door open, Drew paused and looked at her with a puzzled frown. 'What's wrong?'

'My sense of direction, or lack of it, is legendary.'

Drew seemed to accept her explanation. She knew it was cowardly to postpone the inevitable, but she pushed the problem firmly to the back of her mind. It was easy when her mind was crammed full to overflowing with all these new and marvellous sensations; she desperately didn't want to spoil everything now.

'Concentrate. I'm relying on you.'

'I hope I don't disappoint you.' She smiled, but a flicker of anxiety crept once more into her eyes. 'I can walk,' she began, but he was already taking the stairs two at a time, as though he carried nothing more substantial than thistledown.

Dear Lord, Eve, when you start talking thistledown you've gone mushy beyond redemption! What sort of talk was that for a girl with her feet on the ground? Her foot, rubbing up and down the opposite calf, was a pointed reminder that her feet were a long way from the ground, figuratively or otherwise!

'My room's the second door on the left.'

'The point of no return?' Back pressed against her bedroom door, Drew looked directly at her, one eyebrow at a quizzical angle.

He'd obviously picked up on her concerns—with that eerie perception of his—and interpreted them in his own way. A way that had brought a taut strain to his face. *He thinks I'm going to choke at the final fence.*

'That was way…way back,' she said firmly.

He inclined his head slightly and exhaled sharply. 'Good,' he said simply as he leaned back against the door, hard enough to make it swing open. He reached blindly behind him for a light switch, his lips fastened against hers.

Eve was fast discovering there was an infinite variety to kissing. When he came up for air she gave a deep sigh and let her head drop back against his shoulder.

When she and her dad had decorated her room she'd thought the pale pink and grey co-ordination was the last thing in style; it had been the envy of all her friends. She'd been sixteen then, and the style hadn't stood the test of time. Putting it kindly, it looked distinctly frayed around the edges. What would Drew make of her early attempts at interior design?

She lifted her head from his shoulder to see what his reaction would be, only he didn't seem to have much interest in the decor. He had a lot of interest in her, though. He was watching her with an expression of gloating admiration. She'd have had to be made of stone not to be excited by that look. She didn't feel remotely stone-like as she nibbled softly on the fingers he trailed against her mouth.

Walking slap-bang into the side of her bunk bed did eventually distract Drew. He did a quick adjustment that just stopped her being deposited on the inevitably pink quilt. She'd discovered how much she loathed pink about six months after the transformation—just as her mother had predicted; her parents had been great believers in letting the young make their own mistakes—and live with them! Only due to financial restraints she'd been living with her mistakes a lot longer than any of them had anticipated all that time ago.

Drew blinked, as if seeing the room for the first time. 'You like pink?'

'You get used to it eventually.'

She probably spent most of her nights sharing the bearded louse's room. Small wonder she didn't bother redecorating her own space.

His sudden frown had a fastidious edge that made Eve all the more conscious of every shabby piece of bad taste. She stiffened in his arms.

'We could turn out the light,' she conceded, her voice stiff with injured pride, 'if your libido can't take the strain. If you need glamour, scented sheets and candlelight to keep you in the mood we might as well call it a day right now!' she told him bluntly.

He gave a hoarse gasp of strained amusement and lowered her slowly to her feet. The slow part and the hand firmly placed in the small of her back made it impossible for her to survive the process unaware of how unscathed his libido was!

'I've been finding it a problem dampening down my lecherous instincts, not igniting them.' She squirmed against him, but his hand prevented her retreat. 'A big problem,' he added with a wicked glint in his eyes.

Eve was relieved when those remarkable eyes moved beyond her face. Her senses were so highly tuned to every flicker of expression in the azure orbs she had felt completely out of her depth.

Drew was regarding the bunks warily. 'Do you like being on top or underneath?' A grin split his face as her colour deepened to match the colour scheme—bright pink all over.

'I was talking geographically, not technically,' he told her solemnly. 'Though now you come to mention it…'

'I knew that,' she sniffed.

He laughed, and scooped her back up into his arms. Without warning he sat down on the bottom bunk; without warning he pulled Eve across his lap.

'A man could get concussion in the throes of passion,' he observed, frowning upward at the top bunk, which was just a whisper away from the top of his head.

Why? What was he going to do? she wondered, feeling suddenly distinctly out of her depth. 'Drew…' she began worriedly. She didn't finish her words because he'd rolled smoothly onto his side and placed her on the bed.

'Hold that thought, angel. Just let me get out of this.' He began pulling clumsily at his jacket, shrugging it off his powerful shoulders. 'You've been driving me slightly crazy from day one, do you know that? There,' he said, finally managing to shrug off his jacket. 'No surgery required just yet,' he muttered drily, half to himself.

'Surgery?' His shirt was now completely unbuttoned, and the shadowy promise of his body and its sleek, sculpted musculature sent an erotic thrill racing through her veins.

'Private joke.'

'I'm not sure this is the time for secrets,' she prompted, when she realised he couldn't see she was waiting for the punchline. Knowing she could see him but the shadows were hiding her gave her the passing illusion of security. The illusion vanished when he spoke.

'Lottie said my suit would have to be surgically removed by the time I was forty. So maybe I've got a few years' leeway.'

Her sharp intake of breath must have been audible from where he stood because he paused, his hands on the leather belt that circled his waist. Frustrated beyond belief, he strained and failed to see her face in the shadows. All he could make out was a pale blur.

Did he think I wanted to know that? 'Let's get one thing straight right now, Drew. Don't talk about Lottie when you're making love to me.'

His lips formed a silent whistle of relief. It could have been much, *much* worse, he reflected. Under normal circumstances he could handle rejection pretty well—since Lottie he hadn't cared about any woman enough for it to matter. But it would have taken more than a cold shower to solve things if Eve had decided to boot him out, thanks to his tactless reference to an ex-lover.

'I can live with that. Any other conditions I should know about?'

'Don't think about her either.' So what if she sounded like an advocate of the thought police? She didn't even care if the request made her sound revealingly vulnerable. It was vitally important to her to know that even if he didn't love her she wasn't just a substitute tonight. All she'd have at the end of the day was memories, and she didn't want those memories to be flawed.

Did she think he still carried a torch for Lottie? He opened his mouth to reassure her, and closed it. He couldn't bring his ex-flame into the conversation two seconds after promising not to mention her and stay credible.

'The only person I'll be thinking about tonight is you, Eve.' He could have added that she was the only person he'd been thinking about for some time now—especially at night. But he knew that sort of extravagant confession might spook her completely.

Her misplaced sense of loyalty to that creep Theo was obviously putting her through the wringer. Drew had no such guilty qualms where that guy was concerned. He'd taken advantage of a young, vulnerable girl and now he took Eve for granted—he didn't deserve that sort of dedication!

She was so damned trusting, he fumed silently. She deserved more, and he was going to show her what 'more' was all about!

He was having trouble living in harmony with the combination of lust and protectiveness, with a seasoning of frustration throw in, that seemed to be influencing his decisions these days.

His words had had a ring of authenticity but Eve had seen his hesitation. The chill that had settled around her heart didn't thaw immediately.

'You'll have to take my word for it. Do you want me to go?'

'No!'

Eve registered his deep sigh of relief, but she didn't have time to feel smug at all—it had been a very flattering sound, because Drew, minus most of his clothes, had slid in beside her on the narrow bed.

'Love me, Eve,' he murmured huskily. 'I want you to live out your fantasies with me.'

CHAPTER SEVEN

THE knot in her stomach tightened. A paradoxical concoction of dismay and excitement spilled out into the liquid darkness of her wide-eyed gaze. Her breath came in short, shallow gasps.

'Fantasies...?' Her voice emerged as a dry rasp.

'You're right.' His voice, all deep, velvety seduction, reached out to her from the shadows and announced frankly, 'It would be a case of over-stimulation. I'll find out your secrets later. Come here. I can't see your face.'

Later! Not very much later, she thought, just before everything went a little crazy. The arm that slid beneath her just above waist level came to rest in between her shoulder-blades. A little pressure and she was flat up against him. Thigh to thigh, chest to chest. Her chest was sending out messages of exquisite agony as her breasts were squashed up against him. With his free hand he lightly took hold of her left leg behind the knee and looped it high over his hip.

'Here.' He took hold of her hand and guided it to the area where their hips were sealed. 'Help me.'

Under her fingers she felt the arrogant thrust of his male arousal, and her stomach muscles quivered in a series of sharp contractions. The dull ache at the apex of her legs became fierce and demanding. Sexual awareness washed over her in a scalding flood. I'm the one who needs help, she thought, moaning as his tongue stabbed hungrily into her mouth. Eve kissed him back hard enough to send his head back against the pillow.

Now, half sprawled over him, Eve raised her upper body

a little off his and felt for the zip fastening. 'You're so... delicious,' she began fervently.

'How do you know? You haven't tasted me yet.'

She wanted to, though. She stopped pressing feverish little kisses against his neck. How could a person look at that smooth golden skin and not want to touch, taste? Her eyes ran hungrily over his broad chest and flat washboard belly. Knees tucked in either side of his slim hips, she placed both hands flat on his chest, her curling fingers resting lightly on the muscled ridges. Drew seemed content to watch her from under the protective sweep of dark curling lashes.

She let her sultry gaze rest momentarily on his face before bending forward. When she eventually lifted her head she could see the fine quivering movement of his muscles under the sheen of sweat which now bathed his skin.

'Like that?' she asked, running her tongue over her lips. The parts of him she'd sampled tasted pretty marvellous. A sense of voluptuous female power was coursing through her veins as she began to straighten up, intent on completing her original task.

'Watch out!' he yelled suddenly, catching her by the arm and jerking her down.

Eve collapsed onto her elbows on top of him. His arousal dug deeply into the soft flesh of her belly and she gave a small frantic moan. As she lay sprawled untidily on top of him she could feel his ribcage lift and fall dramatically, in time with his rapid inhalations.

His hands moved to the taut curves of her bottom and his fingers slid smoothly beneath the fragile lacy covering to spread warmly over her skin before he removed it completely. He made no attempt to remove her stockings, but caressed her quivering thighs over the fine denier covering.

'Avoid concussion, remember?' he said in her ear. Remember? She didn't even remember her own name!

'Don't stop,' he added urgently, running a shaking hand over her flank. 'You were undressing me.'

'I was?' She pressed her open mouth over the point on his neck where a pulse throbbed. The intimacy of her sweat-slick limbs tangled with his; the smell of their mingled sexual arousal; the stud fastening at his waistband digging into her stomach—it all combined to create a delicious drugged sensual haze.

'Does this refresh your memory?' Fingers interwoven with hers, he dragged her hand downwards. The slight contact made his body jerk in reaction and he surged against her hand. She bit back a cry of pain as his fingers spasmed within hers.

'I want you, Eve Gordon. God, but I want you!' he groaned, turning his head against the pillow and drawing a strangled breath in between clenched teeth. To Eve's fascinated eyes he looked to be in agony. 'Just don't touch me for a minute,' he begged hoarsely.

Not touch him! That was a lot to ask. She wanted to touch him everywhere, in every way. She reached aggressively for the waistband of his pants and tugged hard.

'Will you do something and not just lie there?' she requested in breathless frustration.

Drew looked at the glow of white-hot hunger in her eyes and a grin, fierce and predatory, split his taut features. Eve grew still. His expression was like a fist tightening in her belly. The sexual challenge in his eyes had her inner core reach and exceed melting point in the time it took to gasp. She was on fire. He lifted his hips in a fluid movement and the trousers slid down over his hips and thighs. A quick kick and they were gone. The white jersey boxers he wore followed suit.

Was a girl meant to look? she wondered guiltily as she obeyed her instincts. She gave a little gasp and her mouth fell open.

Hurriedly she raised her eyes, only to collide with his. Her cheeks flamed as he silently mouthed 'thanks'.

'The lady wants action? I think I can comply.' He flipped her over onto her back and gorged himself on the sight of her pale, slender body. 'Like sweet, tight berries,' he said thickly, drawing a slow circle with one finger around the rich pink areola area of the nipple on one full, aching breast. 'A ripe, sweet berry,' he slurred, lifting his head. There were febrile bands of colour high on his finely chis-elled cheekbones.

The moisture from his mouth felt cool against her heated skin. She felt the deep thrum of sexual arousal throb through her body. Was it really her thighs he was parting? she wondered, floating on a wave of sensual detachment.

The earth-shattering sensation as he touched the hot, slick point between her legs had her crashing back to re-ality. The pulse of electrifying pleasure tore through her body and was followed by more equally mind-blowing delight.

Head thrown back, the sinews in her neck grew visibly taut. Her skin glistened with a fine covering of sweat; it pooled in the small valley between her breasts and trickled down her arched back. She let out a lost cry and dug her fingers into the muscular ridges across his shoulders. The pressure would leave bruises, but Drew didn't appear to register the pain.

The look on her face was one of stark appeal when her hot, glazed gaze collided with his. 'Drew…please…' Her fractured whisper was barely audible.

All she felt was deep relief when his body settled over hers. No apprehension, no uneasy recollection to disguise her inexperienced reactions emerged to spoil this perfect moment of imminent fulfilment.

Drew felt the resistance of her body as he thrust deeply upwards. It was too late. His protest emerged as a hoarse,

broken cry before his regret was submerged in a blind rush
of elemental need as she closed tightly around him.

'This feels so good!' Eve gasped in awed pleasure, her
long legs wrapped snugly around him. She flexed her toes
and rotated her slim ankles as every fibre of her being was
drenched in the gratifying sensation of being filled. 'I
thought...' she began. She'd thought there would be pain,
not this glorious, indescribably sweet sensation.

'Sweet mercy!' he breathed hoarsely. His body was
shuddering with the effort it cost him not to obey the compulsion to drive deeper into her warm, receptive body.

'Am I hurting you?' she asked in concern. His face was
the taut mask of someone in agony. Was she doing something wrong? Or not doing something?

'*Hurting me!*' His breath hissed hotly against her breasts
as his head sagged. 'You're the most impossible, irresistible...'

Her hips moved in what she hoped was an encouraging
fashion. 'I like it.' She spread her hands over his tight muscular behind just as his body began to move. Her fingers
tightened convulsively, her nails biting into his flesh as a
series of gasps which got gradually sharper and faster
emerged from her open mouth.

'Oh, you beautiful, beautiful man!' she cried exultantly
as her body reached a shattering climax. She sank back,
delirious with pleasure, and felt the last pulses of his shuddering release inside her.

'Awesome!' she breathed fervently as his head came to
rest on her shoulder. Her fingers curved around the back of
his head, pushing softly into his damp pale hair. She gave
a tiny sigh of pure contentment.

Awesome. His nephew's current favourite adjective. It
effectively put her in a different generation in his mind,
and drove home the enormity of what he'd just done.

If he'd known... Too late now for *ifs* and *buts* he told

himself as the thud of his heart-rate became merely thunderous. It was easy to pretend he'd have acted nobly if he'd known, but he couldn't deny that part of him had experienced a deep, primitive satisfaction to be the first. Another part had been equally appalled. The situation carried responsibilities he didn't want.

Eve watched enchanted as the fine muscles under the gleaming skin of his shoulders still quivered and he lay there breathing hard.

'Why?' he said, without lifting his head.

Eve had her first inkling that all was not well. Oh, no, she thought, just when I wanted to wallow in this taste of paradise.

Play it dumb, she decided. 'Why what?'

'Don't come the innocent with me...only that's exactly what you were!' he accused incredulously. Abruptly he flipped over onto his back and sat up. It would have been a stunning display of co-ordination and animal grace if he hadn't come in direct collision with the metal bedframe above their heads at the last second.

He used a couple of words she wasn't too familiar with and, still clutching his head, rolled off the bed and landed on the inhospitable floor on his knees.

'Why haven't you slept with your bloody professor?' he bellowed, when the waves of agony from his skull had reduced to a dull roar.

'Do you really think Theo is the sort of man who'd sleep with an eighteen-year-old virgin?' She shook her head pityingly. 'Or even a twenty-three-year-old virgin?' she added drily as an afterthought. Drew might be a financial wizard, but he was a really terrible judge of character.

His sick pallor intensified and Eve hoped he hadn't done anything drastic to his head.

'But I am.'

She blinked, not immediately comprehending his words.

'I didn't mean it like that, Drew,' she assured him earnestly. 'I wanted you to sleep with me.'

'And now I know why.' It was ironic that he'd been worried she might feel something special for him. Ironic that he'd almost talked himself into thinking that wasn't necessarily disastrous.

It was Eve's turn to feel sick. He'd guessed that she'd fallen for him, and if his brooding expression was anything to go by he didn't like it.

'You're assuming that the guy has high principles, not just a lack of interest in inexperienced virgins,' he sneered, brushing a hank of sweat-darkened hair from his eyes. 'Or maybe he's impotent!'

'I hope not,' she said, anxiously recalling Theo's errand tonight. Then she sent him a vexed frown. Of course Theo wasn't. She was letting Drew's wild, nasty insinuations get to her. 'That's a very…very bitchy thing to say,' she reproached. 'And I don't know why you're getting so aggravated? It seemed to me you quite enjoyed it, even if I'm not up to your standard!' she pointed out tartly, feeling her indignation rising with each passing second. She couldn't for the life of her understand what all his heavy innuendo was aimed at.

Drew listened to her, his expression growing blacker and more daunting. 'Are you expected to offer proof? Should I sign a statement to confirm you are no longer virginal?'

'Is that common practice?' she asked mildly. Should she call a doctor, or maybe take him straight to the hospital? Could the damage from head injuries be permanent? she fretted.

'Don't ask me. I've never been involved in a ritual deflowering before! Were you already looking for a suitable partner before you met me? Or is this plan a recent creation of your feverish little brain? You must be really besotted with the fool!'

Eve blinked! *Ritual deflowering!* The last piece of the surreal jigsaw slotted into place. He actually thought she'd slept with him to lose her virginity so that Theo would become her lover! She struggled to follow this unlikely leap he'd made. It was just about the craziest theory she'd ever heard!

Ironically, she'd never actually been sure that Drew had swallowed the fake lover story. It had always seemed a bit weak to her. She hadn't known then he had a natural talent for lurid fairy tales!

'I'm not in love with Theo.' She'd blackened the poor man's name for long enough; this had to stop, she decided guiltily. Face-saving was one thing, but this was something entirely more serious—she had to come clean.

'Then why did you tell me he was your boyfriend?'

Yes, Evie, why don't you tell him? she silently jeered. She took a deep breath. She wasn't ready for that quite yet.

'You wanted me to be in love with Theo so that you could have the pleasure of proving you could take me away from him!' she accused, going straight into attack mode. Wasn't that what turned the dominant male on? And Drew was about as dominant as they got! The more she thought about it the more sense this made.

'Why else would you have been so persistent? It's not as if you've been playing hard to get, Drew, so why, if I'd been in such a hurry to callously use your body, would I have held out this long?'

He wiped his hand over his face and she saw the flicker of uncertainty in his eyes. 'Then why did you let me think...?' His eyebrows drew together in a straight line across the bridge of his nose. 'You never tried to put me straight. You knew I thought you were living together.'

'Maybe I didn't think my sex-life, or lack of it, was any of your business. Actually, I didn't mean it to go on this long,' she admitted with a sigh. She gathered the loosened sheet around her and, drawing her knees up to her chest pulled the white cotton up to her chin. 'The first time I didn't think I'd ever see you again, and I created the lover as a sort of defence mechanism, I think. You were looking down your nose at me...all snooty superiority,' she reminded him.

'Theo is a dear friend. He knew Dad and Mum from the university.' Her mother had been a lecturer in the Art department and her father had taught Sociology. 'He's Nick's godfather, for heaven's sake!'

Despite the fact her words had the indisputable ring of truth, Drew couldn't entirely banish the feelings of disbelief. He struggled to hide the wave of mortification that washed over him. He could feel relaxed with his naked state, but a jealous leap of the imagination was a different matter entirely. He'd been ranting like some jealous sucker. His expression grew remote as he reflected on his cringeworthy display. A display that was going to stand out in his memory until his dying day—possibly longer!

'Later on...?' he enquired tightly, as a dull red colour crept under his even, golden tan.

Eve met his eyes with a calm she was far from feeling. His expression suggested he'd lost interest in the subject but she doggedly continued. 'Later I knew about Lottie, that you were still in love with her.' She left a gap just big enough for him to jump in with a hasty denial. His silence was like a knife in the heart. 'I didn't want to be your last fling. I couldn't hide the fact I found you attractive, but I didn't want you to guess I'd fallen in love with you.'

Well, if she'd wanted to enjoy a brief, glorious affair she'd blown it now! Drew had made it plain on more than one occasion that he wasn't into emotional complications. And as complications went...

Eve couldn't feel sorry, though. How could they have gone on with her pretending she didn't want or need commitment and everything that went with it? She felt a wave of relief. Forget about the conventional games a girl was supposed to play; they just didn't come naturally to her. She was by inclination a cards-on-the-table sort of girl. To hell with dignity. There was nothing very dignified in becoming enmeshed in a web of foolish lies.

'What did you say?' His incredulous question broke the moment of stunned silence that had followed her matter-of-fact announcement.

Why the hell hadn't he stuck to women who, like himself, knew how to separate love from sexual gratification? Because he'd wanted *this* woman, and it had been everything he'd imagined it would be and more, he reflected, his mind dwelling with distracting pleasure on their frenzied coupling.

'I think saying it once is enough humiliation to satisfy anyone,' she responded drily.

She hadn't expected to hear her declaration echoed—not outside her dreams—but he was reacting probably marginally worse than she'd expected. He looked as though someone had just kicked him hard in a vital area. She'd been trying so hard to get the better of Drew Cummings, and all it took was the truth, she thought, her lips twisting in a bitter little smile. When he'd expressed a desire to know her secrets he'd obviously had something quite different in mind.

'I didn't know.'

'Well, I haven't known long myself,' she conceded fairly. 'Don't look so worried. I'm not about to turn into some sort of obsessive stalker.'

'Me! It's you I'm worried about! I'd never have taken advantage if...' he yelled irately. He was filled with an urgent desire to shake her. What sort of woman left herself so wide open to abuse, so...defenceless? He already knew the answer, because it was those self-same candid, painfully direct qualities that made Eve different from any other woman he'd ever met—that had attracted him to her.

For one crazy, brief moment he flirted with the dangerously attractive notion of responding to her open avowal positively. He brushed aside the thought angrily. He'd already learnt the hard way what could happen when you fell in love. No, he was going to stick to uncomplicated sex— chemistry—whatever you wanted to call it. After what he'd been through he'd be certifiable to consider anything else— wouldn't he?

'Well, I suppose that's some sort of improvement. A few seconds ago I was the one taking advantage of you.' She sighed and lifted her shoulders fractionally. 'Let's just put this down to experience,' she suggested prosaically.

She blinked, taken aback a little by the increased ferocity of his smouldering glare. He looked as if she'd just made an indecent proposition. Would living with rejection make her a better, stronger person? Eve wished with all her heart that she wasn't going to find out.

She was making this too easy for him, he brooded. He was perfectly aware that his gut reaction was perverse. 'You should have told me,' he growled with an ill-natured scowl.

'Which? The virgin part or the love part?' He was the one who'd wanted to know her secrets. Selective secrets only, it would seem.

'You know I don't want...'

'Love?'

'Complications,' he bit out. 'Do you have to sound so damned chirpy?'

'I can give you a detailed account of my lacerated sensibilities if you prefer?' she retorted tartly. 'Followed by a hysterically uncontrolled outburst. The fact is I'll get over it.' I hope so, she thought fervently. Because this sort of pain, this enormous aching emptiness inside, where very recently she had felt complete for the first time in her adult life—all that on a permanent basis could drive a person insane.

'Of course you will.'

'Like you did with Lottie.' There was a hint of challenge in the stubborn tilt of her chin, compressed lips and over-bright eyes. 'Minus all the cynicism about commitments. A lot of people get hurt, Drew, but they don't let it influence the way they live the rest of their life. As for the playboy role, it does have a natural shelf-life. A man of a certain age starts to look a little pathetic squiring yet another blonde bimbo.'

She knew perfectly well that what Drew had had very little to do with age, and that he was congenitally incapable of looking foolish, but she needed to vent her frustration on someone, and he was the obvious candidate.

'I thought I was the blond bimbo? Blond, grey or bald—I'm sure I can rely on you to tell me when that time has come.'

'I don't think you need to worry on that score,' she told him with a watery smile. 'They do say that sort of thing is genetic, and your father has a full head of hair. You look like him.'

Her voice wobbled, and she dashed an angry hand across her eyes, sniffing hard as she did so. She looked so lost, so alone. Drew experienced an incapacitating desire to take her in his arms and kiss away the tears.

Eve regained control about the same moment he did. She saw he looked as pale and drawn as she felt.

'Well, actually,' she told him bluntly, 'I don't think you're cut out for the playboy role at all.' Eve was convinced he still wanted all the things he'd once had with Lottie—the whole family and responsibility ballgame.

Leaning her chin on her sheet-shrouded knees, she began to rock gently back and forth, her reflective expression tinged with sorrow. She suspected that when he accepted this he'd be back with Lottie faster than the speed of light.

'You get what you see, Eve.' He seemed to have forgotten how much of him she *could* see as he held his arms out wide. Eve looked with longing at his body. He was beautiful. 'Don't make the mistake of imagining I'm anything deeper or more profound.' She'd never heard his voice sound more harsh.

If it was me he loved I'd take some pretty drastic steps to make him wake up to himself. Only it isn't me he loves, she reminded herself brutally.

'Perhaps I should go?' he said heavily.

It sounded better than 'I'm leaving as fast as humanly possible', but it translated just the same. She watched with a heavy heart as he pulled his trousers over his long, long legs and fastened them over his slim, sexy hips.

'Perhaps I should have slept with Theo,' she said, suddenly very angry with him. 'As you're so fastidious about virgins. You had no objections to being the *other* man; it's just being the *first* man you have problems with! For the moment your logic escapes me.'

Unfortunately it didn't. He'd felt it quite safe to conduct a flirtation with a woman who was looking for a bit of extra-curricular excitement. A woman with a much more old-fashioned attitude to love and sex came with the sort of price tag he had no intention of paying.

'It isn't that and you know it, Eve,' he accused quietly. 'You want something I can't give. I wish I could.'

'Do you, Drew?' The anger drained abruptly away from her.

A spasm contorted his features as his glance rested on her wistful face. 'I don't want to buy into all that sentimentality again,' he told her harshly. 'I'm to blame,' he added heavily. 'I accept that. You can't just go giving your heart away like that!' he yelled suddenly. 'You'll get hurt!'

He regarded her with an expression of incredulous fury. Her attitude baffled him completely.

'That's my choice,' she returned with a tight, humourless smile.

Drew looked at her and gave an explosive sigh of disbelief and a muttered curse before he turned his back to her and began to pull on the rest of his clothes.

Eve's eyes narrowed. The frustration and mortification of the situation were eating away at her shredded nerves. She watched him pull on his shirt and fling his jacket over one shoulder; his clear-cut profile was bleak and desolate.

Ought I to be flinging ultimatums at him? Something bold and challenging, like *Go through that door and you'll never see me again*?

On second thoughts she concluded that would be pretty pointless, because never seeing her again was obviously the situation he wanted to achieve.

For a moment Drew stood, hand on the doorhandle, his mobile features clearly displaying an internal conflict. Eve's natural optimism started to re-emerge, and then he said heavily, 'Take care of yourself.'

Because nobody else is going to! she thought, as her slender hopes were thoroughly dashed by his terse words. Tears of self-pity began to seep out from under her eyelids as she threw herself full-stretch on the bed and began to cry in earnest.

Eve had a visitor the following morning. She was still wearing a towelling robe when Katie Beck's face appeared at her kitchen window. Eve yelped, and slopped most of her scalding coffee over her bare legs. She leapt to her feet and yelped again, this time in pain.

'Sorry, I didn't mean to frighten you.' The tall blonde let herself in and looked around the room with unconcealed curiosity. 'I just dropped by to tell you... Alone are you?' she enquired casually.

'Yes, I am.'

'Oh!' Drew's sister looked crestfallen, but she wasn't the sort of person to stay down for long.

'You really should put some cold water on that,' she said, frowning critically at Eve's ineffectual dabs at the pink area on her knee. 'Right away would be best. Have you got anything frozen in here?' She calmly rummaged through Eve's freezer and triumphantly produced a bag of peas. 'Shove these on the burn,' she suggested, dumping the bag in Eve's lap.

Eve did as she was bid automatically. She suspected most people did what Katie Beck suggested. The languid, slightly vague front concealed a very determined, astute personality.

'I'm not really burned.'

'Just slightly singed. But better to err on the side of caution, or so Alan says. Does that feel better?'

There was a growing pool of water on the floor, from where the heat of her knee was thawing the frozen vegetables. 'Yes.' Numb was definitely an improvement.

'Excellent! Now, what was I saying? Yes...about the boys—they've got plans to go fishing with Alan today, if you've no objections. I fail to see the attraction of sub-zero temperatures, rain and a riverbank, but there you go.' She shrugged expressively. 'That's men for you. Feel free to interrupt at any time, won't you?' she said with a slow, lazy smile. 'The general consensus is I ramble.'

'No, I don't mind at all. Do you want a coffee? I was just...'

'Drinking one before I barged in. Actually, I'd love one—still a bit jet lagged today, I'm afraid.' She touched the non-existent shadows beneath her eyes and grimaced. 'As no doubt you can see.'

Actually, Eve couldn't, so she said so. She wouldn't have minded plugging into whatever energy source kept this woman going. She never had managed to get to sleep last night, and just getting out of bed this morning had seemed too much effort.

'Aren't you kind? And I'm not just talking about your tactful blindness to the bags under my eyes. Daniel told me—well, his father actually—about what you and Nick tried to do for him. Strange, isn't it? If he'd been a girl we'd have prepared him from the cradle for the unpalatable fact there are some unpleasant males out there. But because Dan's a boy we let him find out the hard way there are some scary girls too.'

'You're not angry?'

'Angry? Good Lord, no.'

'Your brother…' She couldn't get the word out without a bitter little quiver of her lips. She bit down hard to still the ridiculous tremor. 'He seemed to think you'd be annoyed.'

If Katie had noticed the feeble quaver she tactfully didn't let on, much to Eve's relief. 'Only at myself, for not adequately preparing Dan and for leaving him with Drew.'

'Drew did his best.'

Katie Beck smiled thoughtfully at the fiercely defensive response. 'I never doubted he would,' she said soothingly. 'Drew's not the sort to be half-hearted about anything, but it wasn't really fair to dump him with a teenager. I told him if he wanted to play at being paternal he should start with a younger sample—a baby, say. I'd say he was broody,' she continued, apparently seeing nothing strange in Eve's dramatically fluctuating colour.

'I mean, why choose to spend his precious leave buried out here babysitting his nephew? I'll tell you why. He's had après-ski until it's coming out of his ears! What that boy needs is a bit of reality.'

From the way Drew's sister was looking at her Eve knew that *she* was expected to provide that reality, and what, she reflected wryly, could be more real than my face the morning after the night before?

'He's not in love with me.' This was one fantasy that was far too painful to participate in.

'Wouldn't admit it if he was,' came back the bracing response. 'Drew said you were blunt; I like that. I think you'd be very good for my brother.'

Me blunt? Did Katie appreciate the irony of that statement? she wondered. If I'm ever able to laugh again this conversation will definitely have me in stitches!

'He doesn't.' Eve knew if she let her mind dwell on this inescapable fact she'd start bawling like a baby. She blinked to disperse the moisture that was gathering in her eyes.

'Me and my big mouth. I've upset you. I was just so relieved when I saw you. Ever since I heard that that wretched woman was back on the scene I've been terrified she'd wheedle her way back into his affections. Drew's normally the most level-headed of men, but where that woman's concerned—! You know about the Lottie saga? He told you?'

'I sort of stumbled on it,' Eve admitted gruffly.

'Then you know why he doesn't trust his own heart these days. When I think what she…' She took a deep breath and her lips stretched into a humourless smile. 'Just don't give up on him just yet,' she said, draining the coffee cup in a gulp.

She was walking towards the door when she spotted the black length of cloth attached to a brilliantly coloured azalea. She paused and picked up the tie, then with a smile looped it around Eve's neck.

'I expect you'll see him before me,' she said cheerfully.

A scarlet-faced Eve was still babbling denials, none of

which affected her cat-who-got-the-cream smirk, as her visitor let herself out.

Eve was left feeling as if she'd been hit by a cyclone. The interrogation had been benign, but exhausting. Katie Beck had outgrown bright lights and thumbscrews aeons ago!

If she's looking to me to save her brother from Lottie's clutches she's doomed to disappointment.

Eve ducked behind the willow and, back pressed against the bark, stood there listening to her heartbeat and the sound of the two voices as the couple walked up the driveway a few feet away from her.

Her response to the sound of Lottie's voice seemed to be disturbingly Pavlovian. *I hear it, I hide—feeble!* Actually, she might have coped if it had been just Lottie's voice; it was the combination that had sent her into retreat mode.

There wasn't much evidence of Drew's contribution to the conversation, just the odd gravelly monosyllable interspersed amongst Lottie's bright, bubbling chatter. What a terrible voice the woman had, Eve decided uncharitably as she straightened up and stretched to relieve the knot in her spine.

It had been a month almost to the day since she'd last seen Drew, and almost as long since she'd seen Lottie—who was apparently now staying in the capital with a 'friend'. It seemed their little backwater was too tediously slow for this cosmopolitan sophisticate.

Friend—why am I so shocked? It wasn't as if I didn't suspect, she told herself impatiently. Eve gave a self-mocking grimace and squared her slumped shoulders. Inside, the sinking feeling had progressed to a morass of leaden misery in the pit of her stomach.

She'd told herself afterwards—funny how her life had

acquired a new time-scale: before and after Drew Cummings—that she couldn't dismiss a valuable client on the off-chance she'd see something she didn't like. Now she wasn't so sure.

The brief second she'd had to see him, the one before she'd beat her cowardly retreat, had been enough to reinforce the fact she hadn't got over him. His hair was longer; it had started to curl on the collar of his jacket. He looked taller, leaner, and even more sexily gorgeous than the image she carried in her head. A tidal wave of longing had washed over her in that split second. So much for her sensible efforts to get on with her own life.

Lottie didn't top his shoulder, even in those ridiculous heels she always wore, and his arm had been thrown over her shoulders in a protective gesture that had sent jealous barbs deep into Eve. They still lay there, buried, hurting, but she had control now. With a sigh she made her way back to the kitchen garden and continued to lift the new potatoes she'd grown under cloches.

'I've been sent for the vegetables.'

If she hadn't been wearing two layers of socks inside her sturdy boots Eve might well have speared her toe.

'Oh, dear, have you hurt yourself?'

'Only a flesh wound,' Eve responded lightly. Better try next time, she thought, glancing at the pretty bone china dish in Lottie's hands. 'They're not washed yet, you know,' she explained, under no illusion as to what had inspired this display of domesticity. Lottie wanted to do a bit of judicious salt-rubbing, but Eve was determined that she wasn't going to parade any wounds for the purpose!

She was also willing to bet those beautifully manicured hands had never been near a raw vegetable, let alone an unwashed one in their life. The hands moved now, in a pretty helpless way, and Eve couldn't help but notice how thin was the wrist the heavy gold bracelet jangled against.

The angular bones protruded sharply against her milky skin. Obviously Drew's distaste for clinging had certain significant exceptions. This female was the epitome of clinging helplessness.

She was probably born looking for a male shoulder to lean on, Eve thought scornfully. If I'd been well educated I'd no doubt be able to name the appropriate supplier of each piece of designer clothing, from the strappy shoes to the tailored grey jacket. I hope Drew remembers to leave the price tag on his presents; it's probably the sort of romantic gesture she would appreciate!

Eve's eyes widened as with appalled dismay she realised how bitchy her bitter thoughts had been. She smiled particularly warmly to compensate for this shocking lapse.

'If you give me a minute I'll clean them for you,' she said briskly.

'No hurry,' Lottie said, picking her way over the random stone pathway in Eve's wake. She stepped back hastily as Eve turned on the garden tap and hosed down the potatoes.

'You're a treasure.' Lottie's restless gaze rested on the Thermos and lunchbox propped up on the bench. 'Were you about to have lunch?'

'Just elevenses,' Eve replied, pulling the lid off the airtight container and extending it towards her guest. 'Want a piece?'

Lottie regarded the slab of rich fruitcake with round-eyed horror. She gave a little shudder as she vigorously shook her head. She held a hand to her prettily painted lips and averted her eyes.

Eve, who'd been expecting a polite denial, was a little taken aback by this over the top response. Anyone would think I was handing around arsenic!

'You're probably right; I made it.'

'Are you going to eat *all* of that?' Lottie was looking at her as if she was a fairground freak.

'Probably.'

'Don't you worry—about your weight?' she asked.

Eve frowned, unable to understand this fascination with her diet. 'No.'

'Your mother's worried you'll catch cold, Lottie.'

'Drew, darling, you remember Eve, don't you? I've just been telling her what a treasure she is.' She shot a flirtatious glance up at him as he slipped the coat over her shoulders. The look faded when she saw he was looking directly at the younger girl.

'Yes, I remember Eve.'

'Hello, Drew, how are you?' Her heart had started beating again; she could breathe, smile politely. Inside it was as if she was dying.

Drew ignored her response. His hungry gaze was fixed unblinkingly on her face.

What was he doing? You didn't look at a casual acquaintance like that. She'd done her best—been almost nice to Lottie, hadn't fallen in a heap when she'd seen him, even though she'd wanted to. He was as good as flaunting the fact that he knew her very well indeed.

'Will you be in this afternoon?' There was nothing lover-like about his tone; it was terse to the point of rudeness.

'Yes…no…I don't know.'

'It's not a trick question.'

Eve wasn't so sure about that. She continued to stare back at him with an ambiguous mixture of longing and suspicion on her eyes.

'Make it yes.' He didn't do anything to dress up the order. 'I need…' His chest lifted and his lips twisted in a self-derisive grimace. '*We* need to talk.'

Conscious of Lottie's presence, Eve bit back the blistering retort on her tongue. A quick glance in Lottie's direction revealed the older woman was not enjoying being excluded. Was Lottie so anxious to have Drew back she accepted this sort of casual cruelty?

'I'll be there about two.'

And I won't.

It was almost as if he'd heard her defiant thought as his lips curled in a grim smile. 'I'll wait,' he promised softly.

'But, Drew, darling, you promised to take me to town.' Red nails stroked his sleeve.

'Three then, Eve.' A quick nod and he was gone, with Lottie following in his wake like a puppy.

Am I supposed to be grateful he's fitted me in to his busy schedule at all? she wondered, staring after them. She'd be there, all right, she decided grimly. To put him straight on a few salient details. He might be happy to be the other man, but she wasn't going to be the female version for anyone—not even Drew.

CHAPTER EIGHT

'THE first step…' Drew was saying. He'd repeated this particular piece of advice so many times he found himself varying the inflection each time, like an actor practising his lines. '…Is to admit you need help.'

He frowned slightly as he heard the distant wail of a fire siren. He put the nebulous feeling of unease that trickled like icy water the length of his spine down to the evocative sound.

'That's what Rufus said,' came the lethargic reply. 'He doesn't understand, though. Not like you.'

Drew didn't respond to her melting smile. He didn't want to give Lottie any excuse to think things were ever going back to what they had once been. He was getting familiar with the peevish look that crossed her features.

He'd been told by her anxious parents that she was emotionally vulnerable right now, but that didn't stop her milking the situation for all it was worth. Strange how he'd never noticed before how manipulative she could be—love blindness?

Was it this affliction that had made Eve choose him as her first lover? His jaw tightened. It was always the same. Every gesture he made, every thought he formulated, regardless of how inappropriate the occasion, they led him back to the same place, the same person—*Eve*! Anybody would think that, like her namesake, she was the only woman on earth. *For you she is.* The words rose up to mock his resistance.

'Sounds to me like Rufus is worried as hell about you.' Drew couldn't help but feel sympathy for the husband

154

he'd never met. The glitzy world this television producer inhabited had obviously fostered Lottie's existing insecurities. He was no shrink, but her bulimia and the almost pathological conviction that her husband was having affairs with every young, beautiful female he met—and working on a daytime soap must mean there were plenty of those—had to be connected. He wasn't in a position to know which had come first—the bulimia or the marriage problems. If only she'd agree to speak to someone qualified to judge and help he'd feel much happier.

'He married a size twelve. Why the hell would he want a size six?' He knew by now he was wasting his breath; she didn't seem to be thinking straight.

When her parents had rung him, at their wits' end and begging for his help, he hadn't appreciated how severe the problem was. By now he was painfully conscious that he was totally out of his depth. The more he tried to help, the more clingy and dependent she got.

Lottie gave a brittle laugh. 'There's no such thing as too thin.'

Drew opened his mouth to respond, and at that moment the nebulous feeling of incongruity hit him again. Only this time it was stronger, and more specific. Something was badly wrong. He suddenly pulled the vehicle he was driving to the kerb with a dramatic screech of brakes.

'Whatever's wrong?' Lottie asked in astonishment.

'I don't know…*something*.' How did you begin to describe this spine-chilling sensation? he wondered, stunned by the intensity of the bizarre sense of urgency which gripped him.

'What are you talking about?' came the sulky response.

Drew wished he knew. He'd thought he was being pretty extreme when he'd had acupuncture one time, to relieve the pain after a bad climbing accident. Premonitions came under the totally different heading of seriously weird!

'I need to do something. I'll drop you off here—call for a taxi.'

'You want me to get out?' Her voice rose to a level of shrill incredulity. 'Here?' She looked as though he had proposed abandoning her miles from anywhere, not in a desirable corner of leafy suburbia.

'Yes.'

'Well, really!' Lips compressed, she made a song and dance about getting out while Drew drummed his fingers impatiently against the steering wheel.

He was halfway there before he knew he was heading for Acacia Avenue. Somehow he wasn't surprised to see the fire engine and ambulance parked outside number six. He'd never experienced anything close to the feeling of icy, clammy-palmed dread that lay over him like a shroud as he swung his car onto a neighbour's driveway. He leapt out of the car without turning off the engine.

The noise hit him first, and then the smell. The scene was one of organised chaos: acrid smoke filled the air and the Tarmac beneath his feet was swimming with water. Jets were being aimed at the long, sickly streaks of orange that still shot out from the core of the destruction, but it was obvious that despite their efforts nothing much of the old building was going to be saved. A protective numbness descended over his mind as he saw the shattered panes of the upstairs windows.

The various uniformed officers all seemed to be busy. The ones who weren't seemed intent on stopping his progress. Drew moved forward, weaving like a rugby player through the emergency services.

'It was very foolish—very, *very* foolish.' The fire officer with a helmet tucked under his arm wiped a film of perspiration from his face as he read the riot act to the slender figure seated on the bottom step of the open-doored ambulance.

She held one arm extended as a paramedic placed her hand in what looked like a big plastic bag. Drew could see her other hand had already received similar treatment. A large metal box was perched on her knee; she appeared to be guarding it jealously.

'I'm sorry, really, but the photographs are all we have of Mum and Dad,' she said simply.

'Yes, well.' Looking literally down into the smoke-blackened face—very sweet face—of human tragedy took the edge off his justified anger. 'You never go back into a burning building.'

'Never again,' she confirmed truthfully, just before another bout of coughing gripped her.

'That'll do until we get to the hospital,' the paramedic said, securing the tape at her wrist. 'You must leave this on,' he added, lifting the oxygen mask that hung around her neck into place.

With a grimace she half turned her face away and held up her hand. 'But I feel...' It was at that moment she realised for the first time he was there.

'*Drew!*' No, it was too early. She thought he was a lovely illusion. But when a fresh gust of wind dispersed the thin veil of smoke the phantom didn't vanish with it. She struggled to speak, but the oxygen mask cut off any further comment—which, on reflection, was just as well. In her present state of heightened emotions it might well have been something unguarded and undignified like *My love!*

He always seemed to turn up when she needed rescuing. Only this time he was just a bit too late. She couldn't bring herself to look at the smouldering remnants of her home; the terrible sound as the roof fell in was still echoing in her ears.

'You went in there?' He looked really strange. She noticed at first the odd stiffness of his mobile features, and then it struck her that his pallor was rather extraordinary too. His eyes, fixed on her, had an almost incandescent quality. Every suggestion of a line on his face appeared suddenly to be a deeply gouged groove, bisecting the taut planes of his face. He appeared to have aged ten years since she'd last seen him that morning.

'Only got out about ten seconds before the ceiling collapsed,' the firefighter added for good measure. 'To save a bunch of photos!' He shook his head from side to side in weary disbelief.

She tried to pull the mask from her face, to explain that she hadn't really been reckless, but the paramedic who was urging her up the steps into the ambulance frowned disapprovingly.

'You can talk later to your boyfriend.' He cast a knowledgeable eye over Drew. 'Do you want to come along, sir? We've room.' He was familiar with shock, and he didn't want to be responsible for this guy getting behind a driving wheel.

'No, he's not my boyf…!' Eve protested, anxious to dispel this humiliating mistake at the outset. Her voice emerged as a scratchy raw croak. A single look from the paramedic had her grimacing apologetically and lowering the mask.

The desperation in Eve's voice hadn't been lost on Drew. She'd use her last dying breath to deny all association with me. His brooding regard shot abruptly from Eve to the paramedic, alarm sharply flaring in his eyes. 'She'll be…?'

'Fine in next to no time. She was lucky—just smoke inhalation, and the burns to her hands are fairly superficial. Painful, of course.'

Drew's noncommittal nod didn't begin to reflect the relief which washed over him.

As it was, Drew didn't appear to be in much of a mood to talk, or possibly he was composing a suitably scathing speech about her failings. Eve was such a sorry case she'd probably have welcomed even his censure; she'd missed hearing his voice so much it was plain crazy.

He sat on a stretcher on the opposite side of the ambulance, apparently lost in thought—mostly grim, obviously. He looked in her direction repeatedly, and his expression was not warm and comforting. He looked ready and willing to strangle her.

Probably, she decided gloomily, he was thinking of all the things he could have been doing if he hadn't happened to be driving past at the wrong moment. He was probably cursing his luck, and most likely her too. He wasn't the sort of man to leave a female—any female—in her situation alone, but gallantry and nobility were very time-consuming pursuits for a busy man.

The medical opinion echoed the paramedic's. Observation overnight and then home, so long as she had someone able to take care of her. With her hands temporarily out of commission she'd find things pretty difficult.

Eve, who hated hospitals with a vengeance, solemnly assured the medic she had a supportive network that would knock his socks off.

She was just coming to grips with the immediate practicalities of her situation when a nurse pulled back the curtain. 'She's in here,' she announced cheerfully, before disappearing again.

'I thought you'd gone.' At least she had an excuse to be breathless. His big, broad-shouldered figure was outlined against the incongruous background of the florally patterned curtain. The space that had been cramped seconds before was now frankly claustrophobic. Eve clutched tightly to her oxygen mask as if it was a security blanket. Whatever he was feeling was neatly hidden behind a smooth, sardonic expression.

'Wishful thinking?' Drew suggested drily. 'How long do they expect you to wait down here?' he added, staring critically around the small cubicle before glancing at his watch. He seemed to be restless and on edge—impatient to discharge his tiresome duty.

'I'm waiting for a bed on one of the wards.'

Annoyance flickered over his face. 'You've been here for nearly two hours. I'll go and sort this out...'

'Don't you dare!' she croaked hoarsely. No doubt he was used to the little luxuries supplied by the private health sector; if she'd had the breath she might have explained the realities of the NHS to him. 'If I want a reputation as an awkward patient I can achieve it without any help from you!' Chest heaving from the effort of raising her voice, she took a couple of gulps of oxygen before laying aside the mask.

'I never doubted it,' he responded, with the ghost of a drily humorous lilt in his voice. 'I've contacted Nick...' He held up his hand as her eyes widened in dismay. 'Don't worry; I've told him you'll be fine. Alan's driving over to fetch the boys back early.'

'He was so looking forward to the weekend,' she fretted. 'You shouldn't have...'

'Taken it on myself to inform him that his sister is in hospital and his home is burnt to the ground?' Drew responded with brutal impatience. 'The boy's a man. Give him some credit, Eve. The dry ski-slope is still going to be there next month. Can you imagine how he'd feel if you'd kept him in the dark?'

Eve subsided against the pillows, forced to accept that there was some justification to his argument. 'I sometimes forget...'

'That you considered yourself capable of taking on the care of a thirteen-year-old and supporting you both financially when you were his age?'

'Will you stop finishing my sentences for me?' she gasped crossly. Everyone knew that girls matured a lot faster than boys; there was no comparison between Nick and herself at the same age. Every fibre of her rebelled at the very idea of Nick being forced to accept the responsibilities of a family at his age. 'Anyway, I wasn't going to say that.'

'I'm finishing your sentences, Eve, because you shouldn't be starting any.'

'I'm not going to lie here and let you boss me about.' A fit of coughing did nothing to reinforce the claim of well-being she wished to promote.

'That is exactly what you're going to do,' he announced, in a breathtakingly high-handed manner.

That was what *he* thought. If he imagined that just because she happened to be head over heels in love with him, and he was amazingly gorgeous, she was going to meekly let him organise her, she had news for him.

'I'm sure you've got something better to do.'

'Several somethings,' he agreed.

'I need to…'

'Contact the insurance. Nick gave me the name of your company; things are in hand. Katie and Alan have already offered to have Nick stay with them for the moment.'

As much as she didn't want to start depending on him, Eve was relieved. She'd already come reluctantly to the conclusion that Great-Aunt Emily was the only person she could turn to until her hands were healed, and Great-Aunt Emily's hospitality only extended reluctantly to a male— even if that male was her great-nephew.

Aunt Emily didn't like men of any age or description. The theories in the family to explain away her dislike had been colourful and varied. And she didn't dislike quietly; she did so vociferously and with a passion. She was clever, cranky, cantankerous, and she was their only living relation. For obvious reasons there had never been any question of Aunt Emily taking over Nick's guardianship.

'Thank you.'

'Was that so difficult?'

Eve didn't reply, just shot him a reproachful look from under the sweep of her eyelashes. She frowned, aware that something felt wrong. She blinked twice and let out a wail.

'My eyelashes are gone,' she cried, lifting her hand to the charred remnants. A large tear, the first she'd shed, trickled slowly down her cheek, leaving a trail in the sooty deposits that still blackened her face.

She'd lost her home and belongings, she'd singed her lungs, her hands were a painful mass of raw skin and blisters and here she was crying about her eyelashes, of all things!

Drew felt empathy to the point of pain. Unable to restrain himself, he reached out and touched her hunched shoulder. But her body seemed to curl up even tighter, each muscle and sinew screaming rejection. His jaw tightened to the shattering point. All he could do was wait for her to regain control, and try to do the same himself.

He could tell from her expression when she raised her tear-drenched eyes that she resented the fact he'd witnessed her grief. Independent and proud to the point of derangement. And he wouldn't have her any other way. He actually liked her damned perversity!

Bad timing, he concluded reluctantly. You couldn't misinterpret the animosity spilling from her stiff body. Ironically, when the moment had been right he'd been too stubborn and blind to admit the truth. Now it was time for him to display, a bit belatedly, some sensitivity. You couldn't tell a distraught woman who didn't even want you to touch her that you loved her, that you didn't want to waste another minute not showing her how much.

Eve knew he was wishing himself anywhere but here. No doubt he was wondering if she'd come unscrewed enough to start babbling about loving him again!

He could relax. There had been that danger moment

when he'd patted her on the shoulder. She'd wanted desperately to turn and bury her head against his chest, to feel the warmth and security of his arms for just a few precious minutes. But she'd known deep down that a few minutes of bliss would only make it harder—harder to look at him and talk to him with some semblance of rationality later.

'You're vibrating pity,' she accused hoarsely.

'And you're vibrating paranoia,' he responded calmly. 'Your house has just burnt down, Eve, and if you start flinging abuse at everyone who displays a modicum of sympathy...' His eyes narrowed thoughtfully. 'Or is it just *my* sympathy you can't stomach?'

'Miss Gordon?'

Eve sagged in relief against her pillows at the timely interruption.

'They're ready for you on the ward now.'

The curtains were flung aside and she was whizzed at a trotting pace along the antiseptic-smelling corridors. One surreptitious glance over her shoulder told her Drew wasn't doing anything as uncool as trotting; his long legs were coping in a superior and elegant fashion with the pace. Just watching him move hit the pleasure centre of her brain like a ton of bricks.

'You don't have to come.'

'These people don't know you like I do.' Even though she knew it didn't mean anything she experienced a secret thrill at the implied intimacy of his words. 'I wouldn't be surprised if you're already formulating an escape plan.'

It was a measure of how awful she felt that she wasn't!

'I'll leave you both in peace to say your goodbyes. Not too long, mind you.'

Eve stared without gratitude at the retreating back of the ward sister. The world and his neighbour seemed to have got the wrong idea about Drew. He hadn't done anything to disabuse anyone of their assumptions either. Didn't he realise how humiliating she found it? He'd rejected the role; was play-acting the part of loving partner meant to be some sort of consolation prize?

'I'm sorry if this has been an imposition,' she began primly. 'I'm very grateful...'

The explosive sound that emerged from his throat sliced her words off mid-sentence. Before her startled eyes a steady tide of colour travelled up from his neck until it reached the crests of his sharply prominent cheekbones.

He'd never forget his trip to hell and back when he'd thought...*Imposition!* She'd actually said 'imposition'! Lips pulled back in a snarl, he cursed once, with profound conviction.

'I don't want your gratitude!' he ground out 'I...I thought you were dead.' The hoarse words exploded from his throat.

'That would have simplified matters.' She winced the instant the words tripped flippantly off her tongue. How was she supposed to explain that her unforgivable levity was a defence mechanism? Thinking someone you knew—not someone extra-special, she told herself cautiously—had died in a fire would affect anyone.

He looked at her as if she'd just ripped his soul out and danced all over it. Perhaps someone a *little bit* special? a stubbornly optimistic voice in a corner of her mind whispered.

'Drew?' A tentative smile curved her lips as she extended her bandaged hand. 'Perhaps you care about me after all—just a little?'

There was a short, startled pause during which she screwed her eyes up tight. The last thing she needed to see was pity or embarrassment on his face, for he was surely trying to think up a rejection that wouldn't send her clutching for the oxygen mask. Am I the same woman who wouldn't ask a man for a date? I'm all but begging him to let me bear his children! Clutching at straws didn't begin to describe what she was doing.

'I came as soon as I heard.'

Eve snatched her hand back and looked at Theo with an expression of teary gratitude.

'Are you huggable?' he enquired, looking at her swathed extremities anxiously.

'Always,' she assured him, breaking off to cough noisily.

Drew heard the unspoken *for you* loud and clear. His eyes were a wintry ice-blue in a grim, set face.

'Poor sweetheart,' Theo said affectionately. He kissed the top of her bent head and ran a hand softly over her dirty cheek. At the gentle gesture Eve's eyes filled with tears.

Drew had had the perfect cue and he'd missed it, and now there was someone else supplying the sympathetic shoulder—a much more acceptable shoulder, it would seem, he decided sourly. At first Drew hadn't even recognised the guy, with his smart haircut and casual smart clothes—not a single ethnic stripe or clashing colour to be seen!

He viewed this transformation with deep suspicion. He'd have staked his bank balance that a woman had chosen that outfit—and women only did that sort of thing for men they were involved with in one way or another. The stark contrast between the way Eve accepted this creep's sympathy and his own was not lost on him either.

'Do they know how it started?' Eve asked Theo, who, from the smell of smoke on his clothes, had just come from the scene. Drew had probably been scared to say anything in case she took it as a proposal of marriage, she decided gloomily.

'Not for sure. But the fire investigators think it's most likely an electrical fault. I know the fire alarms were working, because I tested them myself only last week,' Theo said with a puzzled frown.

'I wasn't actually in the house; I was out in the garden.'

'Then how…?' He looked at her injured hands.

'She decided to go inside when the fire was raging,' Drew explained helpfully.

Theo's eyebrows shot up. 'How could you be so…?' Eve's lower lip was beginning to quiver, so he gave her a quick hug instead of a lecture. 'How come he's here?' He regarded Drew with much the same expression with which he would have greeted the bubonic plague.

Eve hadn't spelt it out, but Theo had seen the state she'd been in after the party. This sleaze had loved her and left her. He viewed his presence at her sickbed without any sign of pleasure.

'He was just passing and saw the smoke.'

'I wasn't "just passing",' Drew responded unhelpfully. The tension hiked up several notches above bearable as they glared coldly at one another. Eve didn't think she'd have been flattered even if they *hadn't* both been in love with other women.

'All I need is two men brawling beside my hospital bed to make this a perfect day,' she croaked in weary exasperation. What is it with Drew? He doesn't want me, but he doesn't want anyone else to either! And if Theo returned home with a black eye Sally wouldn't be very pleased.

'Do me a favour, *boys.*' The two six-foot-plus men registered this emphasis with similar feelings of discomfiture. 'Keep a lid on the testosterone or I'll ask the sister to throw the pair of you out!'

'Point taken,' Theo responded with a rueful twinkle as he sat back down on the side of the bed.

Eve started coughing again, and both men exchanged guilty glances.

'I think I'll have to ask you both to leave, gentlemen. Miss Gordon needs rest.'

Eve smiled with gratitude at the ward sister.

'Goodnight.' She closed her eyes firmly on the pair of them. When she opened them again she was alone.

CHAPTER NINE

Eve was surprised and touched when Katie Beck arrived with a worried Nick later that night.

Glancing in the overnight bag she had brought, Eve could see several items of lingerie and clothing that looked much better quality than anything she'd lost in the fire. She had only ever window-shopped in the sort of establishments Katie frequented.

But Eve would have forgone this taste of luxury in an instant if it had meant she could have her possessions back again. Everything she owned, all the memories inextricably mixed up with precious items that had no intrinsic market value—they weren't the sort of things that an insurance policy could replace, and they had gone now. It was hard to take in.

With a sympathetic murmur of, 'Your poor hands,' Katie tipped a few things onto the bed for Eve to inspect. 'I hope they're the right size. I just went by what Drew said.' She appeared to take her brother's familiarity with Eve's bra size as perfectly natural. If Eve had been able to finger the pretty pair of knickers she'd have dropped them like hot coals at that sly little aside.

'I'll reimburse you as soon as the insurance is sorted out.'

Katie waved aside this earnest assurance. 'Now, do say if there's anything I've forgotten and I'll get Drew to fetch it in the morning.'

'Morning?' Eve asked in a fraught tone, deeply suspicious.

Drew's sister was looking at her a bit oddly—in all probability on the wary look-out for signs of further emotional instability, Eve reflected wryly. I haven't exactly been at my most rational when we've met before. On the other hand she was probably accustomed to women being foolish around her brother.

Katie wouldn't have wondered at her anxiety if she had witnessed that cringe-making moment earlier on, when Eve had asked Drew— No, that hadn't been a question, she told herself with scalding contempt; it had been a *plea*! 'Perhaps you care about me after all—*just a little*? Talk about begging for crumbs!

'He told me he's picking you up tomorrow.'

'Really?' Eve responded quietly.

There was no way she was going to face Drew tomorrow and sit through some no doubt carefully constructed brush-off. A sensitive rejection was still a rejection in anyone's language.

Nick returned from his trip to the drinks dispenser and to her relief nobody mentioned Drew again.

Just as they were leaving Eve called Nick back. 'Have you got any money?'

'Sorry, I should have thought,' her brother replied, tipping out the contents of his pockets onto the bed.

'Enough for a taxi—to Aunt Emily's,' she elaborated as he started counting out the copper and silver.

Nick stared. '*Aunt Emily's?* You've got to be joking!' he ejaculated in a horror-struck voice.

'Nick, it'll take me hours just to dress myself for the next couple of days,' she reminded him, holding up her hands. 'Where else do you suggest I go?' They both knew there was nowhere else.

'But I thought Uncle Drew had organised…'

'He's not your uncle Drew, or your long-lost brother, Nick. He's no relation whatever to us and I've no desire to rely on him for anything!' she announced in some agitation.

She wondered if it was her fault that Nick had all but adopted the man! As she considered the things about Drew that might appeal to her brother it was brought home to her how drastically her opinion of him had altered since she'd first met him. She knew now he was no frivolous, over-indulged rich playboy.

She'd provided as much security as she could over the years, but perhaps Nick missed the masculine touch, and Drew did effortlessly manage to project an aura that suggested the biggest problem was just a minor obstacle that could and would be overcome.

She'd have been less concerned for her own mental welfare if her attraction to him could be put down to such practical considerations! Drew was no safe port in a storm for her; he was very deep and dangerous waters!

Nick looked at his sister's hectically flushed face and silently pulled out his wallet. He placed the contents on the bedside table.

'How am I supposed to see you if you're staying with the dragon lady?' he grumbled as she kissed the cheek he proffered. 'When I saw her at Christmas she said I was getting to be just like Dad—and you *know* that wasn't meant as a compliment.'

'Well, I agree with her—and that *is* a compliment. You know her bark's worse than her bite, but I can't cope with the squabbling right now, so don't visit too much. It won't be for long,' she promised mistily. 'Consider your hair ruffled,' she added in a husky whisper.

For Aunt Emily, she was really being quite mellow. Being able to legitimately blame the fire on the shoddy work of the electrician—male, naturally—who had originally wired the house had put her in a cheerful frame of mind.

Considering the house hadn't been rewired since her grandparents had moved in, in the early fifties, this wasn't an entirely fair assessment, but Eve hadn't tried to dissuade the old lady.

Aunt Emily had even gone as far as to say she quite enjoyed having Eve around—even if she did expect to be waited on hand and foot. Eve might have felt guiltier if Aunt Emily hadn't had a housekeeper who would have walked through flood and fire to spare the old lady any extra burden her presence might create.

That mellow mood had, of course, been before the man arrived. '*Demanding* I let him in, Eve,' she recounted with a dry chuckle over after-dinner sherry.

Eve, who'd fallen asleep in the conservatory watching the first few flakes of snow fall that afternoon, could see her aunt felt quite rejuvenated by the encounter. Eve was sure she scented her brother's hand in this. Poor Theo—what a cruel trick to play. She'd have to ring him and apologise.

'He said you *wanted* to see him. Let me tell you I put him right there!'

'I'm sure you did, Aunt Emily.'

'He tried to be smarmy then, but I was onto him. I never did trust blue eyes...'

Her heart stopped before exploding into frantic activity. Blue eyes, she thought as it battered against her ribcage; that ruled out Theo and left only one obvious candidate... 'Did he have blond hair, Aunt Emmy? And tall—was he very tall?'

'Yes, and extremely shifty eyes.'

'You sent him away?' Eve got agitatedly to her feet, almost knocking over her sherry glass. She couldn't lose him—she had never had him—but that didn't lessen the profound sense of loss which quite suddenly assailed her. Irrational as it was, the news that Drew had been here and she hadn't even seen him cracked her fragile composure wide open.

'Good God, girl! You're not *crying*, are you?'

'Yes.' The reply came out sullenly defiant. Tears dripped unchecked and silent down her smooth cheeks.

'Over that man?' the old lady enquired, rapping the silver-topped cane she carried for effect rather than necessity on the woodblock floor.

'Yes.'

'I thought you had more sense, girl.'

'So did I!' Eve shouted back. 'But sense isn't a factor when you fall in love. I used to think it was, but now I know different. You could have the misfortune to fall in love with the most despicable person in the world, but I haven't. Drew is...' She took a deep breath, relishing the sound of his name on her tongue. 'Drew is a warm, funny, *lovely* man,' she declared huskily.

'Well *really*!' Emily hardly recognised her prosaically practical niece in the guise of the fervent, glowing creature opposite.

'And he doesn't love me.'

'Then why, might I ask, miss, did he turn up here and demand to see you—*urgently*?'

Eve's head felt as if it might explode. Her chest felt so tight she could almost see the constricting bands of steel clamped there. 'I'll never know now, will I.'

The old lady looked at Eve's dejected posture and tear-drowned eyes and gave a grunt of disgust. 'I thought you had more backbone, Eve,' she sniffed. 'Well, if that young man can be put off by an old lady like me he's not worth having,' she observed acerbically.

'You think he might come back?'

'You know, I suppose, that you look like a rabbit about to jump, ready skinned, into the poacher's sack?'

'Drew isn't...'

'I know—he's *lovely*.' Despite the fact her great-aunt delivered the line with mocking relish there was a hint of unexpected softness in her lined face. 'You know, of course, I won't leave you my money if you marry that big, brawny hunk?'

Eve sank back down into her seat, feeling exhausted and embarrassed in equal parts by her emotional outburst. There wasn't much chance of that happening, was there? She was going to end up rich and lonely.

'I didn't know you were going to.'

'I shall distribute it amongst worthy causes.'

'To further the cause of female emancipation?' Eve suggested with a wryly affectionate smile.

Eve had been learning a lot about the pitfalls of emancipation lately—arranged marriages *had* to be less traumatic than letting your heart do the choosing! But despite her ironic reflections, she was conscious that she owed women like Emily, who had vigorously fought the system, a deep debt of gratitude.

'Fat lot of good it will do when silly girls like you lose their heads over the first pretty face they come across. Is it just sex with this man, or do you actually love him?'

Eve was startled by the octogenarian's blunt question. She raised her dismay-filled eyes to her aunt's face.

The old lady gave a deep, wicked chuckle. 'Your generation didn't invent sex, you know. I was never a prude. In fact in my day I was considered quite... But I won't bore you.'

'I don't think you'd bore me.'

'But I might just shock you,' she responded drily. 'You're just as squeamish as that soft mother of yours— earth mother material.'

'My mother was...' Eve began indignantly.

Emily's wrinkled but still elegant hands made a sharp placatory gesture. 'Your foolish father was a very fortunate man—I know that. You haven't answered my question, girl!' She rapped her cane imperatively against Eve's chair.

'I love him so much it hurts.' Surprisingly there was no scathing response to this blunt declaration. She wouldn't have cared if there had been.

'Then what are you going to do about it?'

'Do?'

Emily gave a snort of exasperation. 'I blame dolls.'

Mine are all gone! A sob bubbled up in Eve's throat. All her old dolls had been boxed up along with other childish mementoes in the attic; they'd all been reduced to ashes now. The evocative image was somehow symbolic of all the other things the fire had swept away.

'What's wrong now?'

Emily didn't reply. Her aunt, a life-long advocate of the stiff upper lip, was uncomfortable with overt displays of emotion. If she had confessed she was crying over old dolls Emily would have thought she'd flipped completely!

Much later, Eve was lying restlessly in bed when she heard the first noise. It was an old house; there were always noises in an old house and she didn't take much notice. She glanced at the clock on the bedside table and after a quick mental calculation took two of the painkillers the hospital had prescribed. The fact she was long overdue the medication was obviously the reason for the throbbing pain in her hands. She wished all pains were so easy to control.

She flicked off the bedside light, hoping she'd be able to settle soon.

This time when she heard the noise she knew for certain it was coming from outside—outside her window, to be precise.

Not being a girl of a nervous disposition, she didn't do anything of a dramatic nature. Screaming was the last thing on her mind as she got out of bed; she just wanted to find out what was making that odd muffled sound.

She pulled apart the heavy brocade drapes at the deep

Georgian sash window. It wasn't easy to open the window without hurting her fingers, but with a lot of care and a modicum of cursing she managed it. The icy air rushed into the room, as did a flurry of snow, and the wind pinned the light lawn shift she wore against her body. Braving the cold, she thrust her head out of the window. The early spring bulbs tempted out by the previous week's warmth were now shrouded in a white blanket. The white world was eerily silent, all the night sounds muffled—well, not quite all. There was a grating sound on the wall below her.

The dark-clad figure was not well camouflaged against the stone wall. 'I've called the police!' she yelled down.

The figure, which had been moving with cat-like agility, lurched suddenly to one side at the sound of her voice. Eve gave a sigh of relief when he steadied. He looked up, and Eve felt the sense of unreality deepen.

'What are you doing here?'

'What does it look like?' came the slightly breathless reply.

To Eve's horrorstruck eyes it looked as if Drew was clinging to the seamless smoothness of a sandstone wall at least twenty feet above the ground—ground that, though covered with white fluffy snow at the moment, was hard, unforgiving cobbles underneath.

Her eyes frantically searched in vain for anything bearing a remote resemblance to a hand or foothold. Any minute now he was going to fall.

Eve only realised she must have voiced her concerns out loud when he impatiently replied, 'No, I'm not.' He sounded quite put out at her lack of confidence in his ability. 'Stand back,' he instructed tersely as his slow but smooth ascent brought him within a head's breadth from her window.

Eve did as she was bid, and a few seconds later his elbows were on the stone sill. With a small grunt he heaved himself through the space and landed with all the grace and balance of a gymnast on the balls of his feet. He straightened up to his full height, shook the snow from his hair and looked curiously around the William-Morris inspired room before calmly closing the window.

Eve had revised the calm part by the time his blue eyes came to rest on her face. Although there was a measured deliberation about his actions there was also a tangible air of barely suppressed tension. He looked to be in the grip of an adrenalin overdose. Perhaps, she pondered angrily, he enjoyed the buzz of risking his skin.

'You look as though you've done this before.'

Dressed all in black, he had a very lean, dangerous look about him. They hadn't said anything about hallucinations when she'd been prescribed the painkillers. Besides, her goosebumps felt pretty realistic, she decided, rubbing the cold flesh of her bare arms.

'You know you're in the worst possible room—access-wise.' He peeled off a pair of black leather gloves and flexed his long fingers.

The fact he was looking hungrily at her made the laconic criticism easier to live with than it should have been.

'If I'd known you intended to climb up to my balcony I'd asked to be moved.' There was snow on the tips of his sooty black eyelashes, and as she stared it began to melt.

'Now a balcony would have made it a lot easier,' he conceded with an edgy grin.

Eve's blasé façade wavered and vanished abruptly. '*How could you?*' she cried. 'It was so irresponsible. You could have *died*.' The fear rose up again, suffocating and thick, obscuring every other sensation but that of visceral dread.

'*Me* irresponsible!' His mouth opened and shut again with a snap. 'How,' he enquired, forcing himself to speak slowly, 'how do you think I felt at the fire, when I discovered you'd actually been back inside?' His voice was raw. 'I thought I'd lost you, Eve.' His eyes had a dark, haunted quality she couldn't quite believe was real.

'That was different,' she began cautiously.

'How different?' he asked, running his fingers through his hair and rubbing the cold excess moisture that covered his hands across his face, as though he needed the icy contact to concentrate his mind. 'I knew you needed me and I thought I was too late.' His expression had a distant, unfocused quality she found scary.

'I don't understand.'

He laughed at that, a harsh, mocking sound. 'You think I do? I only know I was halfway across town when I knew you were in danger. Laugh,' he advised harshly. 'I would if the situation was reversed.'

Eve wasn't laughing, but she was having a hard time accepting the implications of his incredible statement.

'Don't take another step!' she cried urgently, taking two hasty steps back for his one purposeful stride forward. 'Not until you tell me why you felt it necessary to break into my aunt's house in the middle of the night.'

'Because she wouldn't let me in when I came earlier. The situation seemed to call for a crude but effective approach.' He sounded weary, and impatient that she was making him explain the obvious.

He made it sound so perfectly logical that she would have laughed had it been an option. At that precise moment her throat felt oddly achy and tight, and she was having trouble with the most basic of tasks—like swallowing.

He took a step forward and, encouraged by Eve's mute state, took a couple more. 'I couldn't force my way in earlier. She looked so frail; I didn't want to be responsible for her heart giving out or anything.'

'Aunt Emily's not as fragile as she looks,' Eve breathed hoarsely. Her head was spinning. You didn't climb up a

sheer stone wall to give someone the brush-off—*did you?*
'How did you know this was my room?'

'I've been waiting.' He gestured towards the window.
'Over in the woods.'

'Watching the house!'

'With binoculars.'

'With binoculars!' she squeaked incredulously. At what
stage tonight had she finally closed the drapes? Before or
after she'd taken off her clothes? 'Were you fulfilling some
boyhood dream of being a secret agent, or have you always
had criminal tendencies?'

'Only since I've known you, my love.' A tender, rueful
smile tugged at the corners of his mouth.

Eve began to shake more than she had when exposed to
the chill East wind outside. 'Don't call me that.' She
couldn't bear casual endearments—not from him.

'Why not? You are a love, and I've every intention of
making you mine.' His smouldering gaze ran restlessly over
her face. 'Do you have a problem with that?' Some of the
belligerent arrogance faded from his face. 'Tell me I've not
blown this completely, Eve.'

Drew, *pleading*? She could hardly believe what she was
hearing. It *was* a plea, and, if she was any judge, one from
the heart.

'Blown what?' she queried cautiously. If she'd got the
wrong end of the stick here she could make all sorts of a
fool of herself. A bit late to be squeamish about that sort
of thing, but she did have a vested interest in his reply.

'My chances with you!' The words emerged explosively.

'I don't know how or why this is happening, but I'm
really not up to playing hard to get!' With a strangled sob
she took a stumbling step straight into his open arms.

'Oh, Evie!' he breathed, closing his eyes tight and bury-
ing his face in her hair. He could feel the warmth of her
slim body through the fine fabric of her nightgown. 'I love

you. This last month has been pure hell without you. I wouldn't have blamed you if you had turned to Theo after I'd walked...' He omitted the fact his understanding wouldn't have stretched as far as Theo.

'Sally wouldn't have liked that.' She felt the shudder of relief that quivered through his body.

'He's got a Sally? Fantastic. I'm happy for the guy,' Drew breathed magnanimously.

As lovely as it felt to be cradled in his arms, to smell the warm, musky male scent of his body, she forced herself to respond to this husky declaration.

'You can't be in love with me,' she explained to him sadly.

His hand lifted her chin until she had no option but to look directly into his eyes. They were warm, but fierce; greedy, but tender. They were everything she'd ever dreamed of, and much, *much* more.

'Lottie?' he asked.

Eve felt the tears form as she nodded her head vigorously.

'Can I show you something?'

Eve's face showed first confusion and then anger as he pushed a snapshot under her nose. Her misty vision made out his tall, laughing figure standing on a beach, and the smaller, feminine one beside him.

'You came here to show me your holiday snaps?' she squealed in hurt outrage. She would have pulled away but he refused to let her go. 'Do you keep it next to your heart?'

'Look properly,' he insisted urgently.

Eve shot him a glare of furious reproach before doing as he requested. 'Nice tan...' she began acidly, then she saw, and looked again, not quite believing her eyes. 'She's...'

'That's what Lottie looked like when I knew her,' he said quietly, in reply to her confused appeal.

The figure in the snapshot wearing the bikini was pretty, petite—and lushly curvaceous.

'It had been two years. I wondered how I'd feel when we met again—if there'd be anything left of the anger, bitterness, and, yes, love. This was something I wasn't prepared for; it was quite a shock.'

'I had a friend at school who had anorexia,' Eve said, her eyes soft with sympathy.

Drew nodded and pushed the snapshot back into his pocket. 'Her parents tell me it's bulimia. They discovered about it the hard way.' He grimaced, and Eve didn't ask for details. 'They asked me to persuade her to get help— professional help. I couldn't refuse. There is nothing left between us, Eve.'

'She must be very unhappy.' Was it legal to feel this happy? she wondered breathlessly.

'Yes, but not because she left me. She was right about that. Marrying me would have been a disaster,' he mused thoughtfully. 'Meeting you made me see at last all the things that were missing in that relationship. I feel things with you that I didn't know existed before.' His expression was agonised rather than overjoyed as his eyes raked her upturned face.

She couldn't believe that she was responsible for the expression on this strong, powerful man's face. He wasn't making any attempt to hide his vulnerability from her.

'The only thing you seemed to be feeling when I was impolite enough to admit I loved you was the urgent desire to escape!' she protested half-heartedly. She was already ninety-nine per cent convinced by the sheer intensity of Drew's conviction, but the sceptical one per cent needed a little bit more persuading.

'I was too damned scared to admit, even to myself, that I was falling—' He broke off, and visibly fought to control his feelings. Eve watched his chest heave and felt the steady thud of his heartbeat as he regained command. She reached up to touch his hair, but he caught her wrist.

'Poor hand,' he said softly, before kissing the inner aspect of her wrist. 'I was falling in love with this beautiful, crazy girl who said exactly what she was thinking; who drove me to distraction from the moment I laid eyes on her; who didn't give a damn what anyone, least of all me, thought of her…!'

'I care quite a lot what you think of me,' she confessed huskily.

'I think you're the best thing that has ever happened to me, Eve Gordon. I've been the world's worst idiot for not admitting it before.' He kissed her once then, a hard and hungry kiss. He pulled away with a sigh, but his hands lingered either side of her face.

'I made this stupid vow when Lottie dumped me. The predictable, boring sort of vow that involves a lifetime's avoidance of emotional entanglement,' he recounted with a self-derisive sneer. 'It was the coward's route, and I was doing quite well at it too—until this tall, sexy brunette appeared.'

Eve's face went pink with pleasure. *'Me?'* There was a sheen of unshed tears in her eyes.

Some of the strain momentarily drained from his face. He made an elaborate display of looking around the room. 'I don't see any other sexy brunettes here.' His expression sobered as he spoke with slow, condemning deliberation.

'I was like a man on a mission trying to get you into my bed. I used every shameless trick in the book,' he said harshly. 'Rationalising everything I did by telling myself you'd be better off without Theo—that I was helping you break free of him. All the rationalising in the world couldn't prevent me seeing how bloody selfish I'd been when I discovered you'd not had another lover.'

'You make me sound like some credulous little idiot!'

she complained lovingly. 'I knew you didn't love me,
Drew—'

'But I did!' he cut in fiercely. 'Almost from the outset.
I tried hard not to…' he confessed wryly.

'And are you still trying now?' she asked gruffly.

'I was hoping my dramatic entrance might give you a
clue.'

'It nearly gave me a heart attack.' Her unscathed heart
was there in her misty eyes for him to see.

'Does that mean you're not going to make me leave by
the same route?' His arms tightened around her waist as
she stretched up to press her soft lips against his. They were
cold, but it didn't take long before they began to warm.
Her body pressed against his initiated other even more sat-
isfactory changes.

'I'm not going to make you leave at all,' she responded
eventually, with typical candour.

His wide grin became frankly wicked. 'That looks a big
improvement on your bunk beds.' His eyes touched the big,
old-fashioned brass-framed bed.

Eve's eyes dropped self-consciously from his, and when
he touched the nape of her neck he could feel her tension.
'Is something wrong? God, I hurt you, didn't I?' he groaned
hoarsely. 'I was afraid of something like this. Don't let it
put you off. It's better the second time, I promise, love.'

She lifted her face and pressed a finger to his lips. 'No,
no,' she said, stemming the steady flow of self-
recrimination. 'I'm not sure whether something's wrong. It
sort of depends on your point of view,' she explained awkwardly. 'You know those concerns you had about your fad-
ing powers of fertility. Don't worry.'

Drew stared back at her blankly. Then, as she watched,
incredulity crept slowly into his face, followed closely by
delight. His chest swelled, his lips moved, but he couldn't
form the words.

Eve gave a sigh of relief—which was short-lived. Drew suddenly frowned.

'Are you sure? I used...' Was that a tinge of hope she heard in his voice? she wondered dully.

'You must be super-fertile,' she told him grimly.

The pleasure had faded completely from his face. 'I'm so sorry, Eve,' he said heavily. 'I know this isn't what you want. You've only just escaped domestic responsibilities and I'm lumbering you with a baby. You wanted to travel... I wanted to show you all the places...'

Her face cleared. Didn't he know how much she wanted his baby?

'Drew Cummings, I'm having a baby, not entering a nunnery. I've every intention of travelling, and doing all the things I've ever planned, only there'll be three of us now—not two.'

'You're sure?'

'One hundred and ten per cent,' she said firmly. 'Come here,' she said, grabbing a handful of his jumper. She winced.

'Be careful,' he pleaded. 'You don't need the rough stuff. I'll come willingly,' he whispered, pressing his face to hers.

'I just want to demonstrate how sure I am, Drew.'

'Let the lesson begin. And in case you're wondering, Eve, that was a request.'

The kitten, happy to find a nocturnal companion, danced around her ankles. Emily shooed it away. She found she needed little sleep these days. She saw the light under her niece's door and very quietly pushed it open. There was no sound but that of steady breathing in the room. She placed the worn leather journal on the bureau before moving closer to the bed.

Her real legacy to her great-niece lay in those pages, not in the accumulation of possessions she'd amassed over the years. She hoped the girl would not judge her too harshly from what she read in the diary. But most of all she hoped she'd learn from her mistakes and avoid them herself. She had never intended anyone should read it until she was gone, but tonight, seeing Eve's distress and fearing history was about to repeat itself, had made her appreciate that the right time was now.

She was aware of eyes watching her just before she saw the extra occupant in the bed. Eve lay fast asleep, her face rosy with the warm flush of youth, her head resting on the shoulder of the blond-haired Adonis she'd sent away earlier.

Drew raised a stern warning finger to his lips and glanced across quickly at the sleeping figure in his arms. If Emily hadn't seen the loving glow in his eyes when they'd rested on Eve she might well have chastised him for such outrageous impudence.

Not such a wimp after all, she conceded. She would ask him in the morning how he'd managed to get in. Perhaps he could give her some advice on updating her security. He was cool; she'd give him that much, she decided as he met her sharp stare unflinchingly. And there was a humour and intelligence in that look that took the edge off his arrogance.

Drew exhaled deeply as the old lady, her posture youthfully upright, turned and walked away. She hadn't even so much as blinked at finding a naked man in her house—in her great-niece's bed! They certainly bred the women in this family strong and proud. He watched as Aunt Emily paused to pick up the mysterious leatherbound book and tuck it under her arm, throwing a last enigmatic smile over her shoulder as she left.

Eve moved sinuously against him in her sleep. The unexpected visitation was pushed to the back of Drew's mind as he looked down at the woman in his arms. He had no intention of sleeping tonight. Only a fool would sleep when he could look at Eve's face. The deep, unambiguous contentment of his smile didn't stop at the softened contours of his face, it went bone-deep.

When Eve woke the next morning Drew was watching her. 'How long have you been awake?' she asked sleepily.

'I might never sleep again—I'm on a high.' His pulse quickened as he watched her stretch luxuriously. The sensuous little wriggle of her hips made the blood pound deafeningly in his ears.

She gave a little gloating chuckle as the seductive warmth in his expression enfolded her in their own private paradise.

'My love,' she said with mock gravity, 'you're going to need your rest. If, that is, you're going to keep me satisfied.'

'I'd not thought of it in those terms,' he admitted thoughtfully.

The sultry smile died abruptly from Eve's lips. 'How am I going to explain to Aunt Emily that you've spent the night here?' she gasped in horror.

'Oh, I think she'll cope,' he announced casually.

'You don't know Aunt...' She broke off and gave a deep, wicked chuckle as his blond head disappeared beneath the sheets.

'Do you think I might manage to keep you satisfied?' he asked, much later.

Eve responded to the arrogant challenge of his smug grin with a smile of her own, one of deep contentment. 'I'll let you know when I have any complaints,' she assured him with lecherous gravity. Not now or ever, she added silently, looking at the beautiful man beside her.

The world's bestselling romance series.

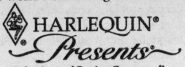

HARLEQUIN®
Presents
Seduction and Passion Guaranteed!

Legally wed,
Great together in bed,
But he's never said…
"I love you"

They're…

Wedlocked!

**The series
where marriages
are made in
haste…and love
comes later….**

Don't miss
HIS CONVENIENT MARRIAGE by Sara Craven #2417
on sale September 2004

Coming soon
MISTRESS TO HER HUSBAND by Penny Jordan #2421
on sale October 2004

**Pick up a Harlequin Presents® novel and you will
enter a world of spine-tingling passion and
provocative, tantalizing romance!**

Available wherever Harlequin books are sold.

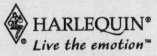

HARLEQUIN®
Live the emotion™

The world's bestselling romance series.

HARLEQUIN®
Presents

Seduction and Passion Guaranteed!

We are pleased to announce
Sandra Marton's fantastic new series

In order to marry, they've got to gamble on love!

Don't miss...
KEIR O'CONNELL'S MISTRESS

Keir O'Connell knew it was time to leave Las Vegas when he became consumed with desire for a dancer. The heat of the desert must have addled his brain! He headed east and set himself up in business—but thoughts of the dancing girl wouldn't leave his head. And then one day there she was, Cassie...

Harlequin Presents #2309
On sale March 2003

Pick up a Harlequin Presents® novel and you will enter a world of spine-tingling passion and provocative, tantalizing romance!

Available wherever Harlequin books are sold.

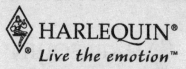

HARLEQUIN®
Live the emotion™

Visit us at www.eHarlequin.com

The world's bestselling romance series.

HARLEQUIN®
Presents

Seduction and Passion Guaranteed!

THE PRINCESS BRIDES

For duty, for money…for passion!

Discover a thrilling new trilogy from a rising star of Harlequin Presents®, Jane Porter!

Meet the Royals…

Chantal, Nicolette and Joelle are members of the blue-blooded Ducasse family. Step inside their sophisticated and glamorous world and watch as these beautiful princesses find they have to marry three international playboys—for duty, for money… and definitely for passion!

Don't miss

THE SULTAN'S BOUGHT BRIDE (#2418)
September 2004

THE GREEK'S ROYAL MISTRESS (#2424)
October 2004

THE ITALIAN'S VIRGIN PRINCESS (#2430)
November 2004

Pick up a Harlequin Presents® novel and you will enter a world of spine-tingling passion and provocative, tantalizing romance!

Available wherever Harlequin books are sold.

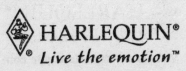

HARLEQUIN®
Live the emotion™

www.eHarlequin.com

HPPBJPOR

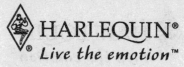

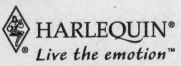

The world's bestselling romance series.

HARLEQUIN®
Presents

Seduction and Passion Guaranteed!

Your dream ticket to the vacation of a lifetime!

Why not relax and allow Harlequin Presents® to whisk you away
to stunning international locations with our new miniseries...

*Where irresistible men and sophisticated women
surrender to seduction under the golden sun.*

**Don't miss this opportunity to experience glamorous
lifestyles and exotic settings in:**

This Month:
MISTRESS OF CONVENIENCE
by Penny Jordan
on sale August 2004, #2409

Coming Next Month:
IN THE ITALIAN'S BED
by Anne Mather
on sale September 2004, #2416

Don't Miss!
THE MISTRESS WIFE
by Lynne Graham
on sale November 2004, #2428

FOREIGN AFFAIRS... A world full of passion!

**Pick up a Harlequin Presents® novel and you will enter a world
of spine-tingling passion and provocative, tantalizing romance!**

Available wherever Harlequin books are sold.

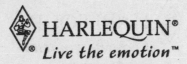

HARLEQUIN®
Live the emotion™

www.eHarlequin.com   HPFAUPD